AN OUTLAW'S CHRISTMAS

A McKettricks of Texas Novel

LINDA LAEL MILLER

AN OUTLAW'S CHRISTMAS

A McKettricks of Texas Novel

Doubleday Large Print
Home Library Edition

HARLEQUIN®

entertain, enrich, inspire™

This edition published by arrangement with Harlequin
Books S.A.

ISBN 978-1-62090-483-1

® and TM are trademarks of Harlequin Enterprises
Limited or its corporate affiliates. Trademarks indicated
with ® are registered in the United States Patent and
Trademark Office, the Canadian Trade Marks Office
and in other countries.

Printed in U.S.A.

**This Large Print Book carries the
Seal of Approval of N.A.V.H.**

Dear Reader,

Welcome back to Blue River, Texas, original home of the McKettricks of Texas and the setting for Clay and Dara Rose's story, *A Lawman's Christmas.*

The year is 1915, and most folks suspect that handsome Sawyer McKettrick, Clay's rowdy cousin, is an outlaw on the run, so it's ironic that he's come to town to take over as marshal, now that Clay is busy running a ranch and starting a family.

Sawyer wasn't sure of his welcome, but he wasn't expecting to be greeted with a bullet, either. Wounded, he finds help—and the lovely Piper St. James—at the one-room schoolhouse.

Piper, the schoolmarm, isn't eager to take in a stranger, especially a bleeding one, but honor and compassion win out, and she looks after Sawyer *and* his horse.

Love is certainly the furthest thing from Piper's mind, and Sawyer's, too, but Christmas has a magic all its own.

May you be blessed this season and always.

In loving memory of Dale Macomber.
Knowing you was a gift I'll always be grateful for.

CHAPTER 1

December, 1915

All but hidden behind a rapidly thickening veil of snow that cold afternoon, Blue River, Texas, looked more like a faint pencil sketch against a gray-and-white background than a real town, constructed of beams and mortar and weathered wood and occupied by flesh-and-blood folks. Squinting against the dense flurries, Sawyer McKettrick could just make out the pitch of a roof or two, the mounded lines of hitching rails and horse troughs, the crooked jut of the occasional chimney. Here and there, the light of a lamp or lantern glowed through the gloom, but as far as Sawyer could tell, nobody was stirring along the sidewalks or traveling the single wide street curving away from the tiny railroad depot.

Beside him, his buckskin gelding, Cherokee, nickered and tossed his big head, no doubt relieved to finally plant four sturdy hooves on solid ground after long hours spent rattling over the rails in a livestock car. Sawyer's own journey, sitting bolt upright on a hard and sooty seat in the near-empty passenger section, had been so dull and so uncomfortable that he probably would have been happier riding with the horse.

Naturally, Cherokee didn't hold up his end of a conversation, but he was a fine listener and a trustworthy companion.

Now, the engineer's whistle sounded a long, plaintive hoot of fare-thee-well behind them, and the train clanked slowly out of the station, iron screeching against iron, steam hissing into the freezing air.

They waited, man and horse, until the sounds grew muffled and distant, though for what, Sawyer couldn't have said. He hadn't expected to be met at the depot—Clay McKettrick, his cousin and closest friend, lived on a ranch several miles outside of Blue River and, given the weather, the trail winding between there and town must be nigh on impassable—but just the same, a momentary sense of loneliness howled through him like a wind scouring the walls of a canyon.

With a glance back at the station, where he'd left his trunk of belongings behind, meaning to fetch it later, Sawyer swung up into the saddle and spoke a gruff, soothing word of encouragement to the horse.

There was a hotel in Blue River—he'd stayed there on his last visit—but he wanted to let Cherokee walk off some stiffness before settling him in over at the livery stable with plenty of hay and a ration of grain, and then making his way back to rent a room. Once he'd secured a bed for the night, he'd send somebody for his trunk, consume a steak dinner in the hotel dining room, and, later on, take a bath and shave.

In the meantime, though, he wanted to attend to his horse. Sawyer gave the animal his head, let him forge his own way, at his own pace, through the deep snow and the unnerving silence.

The buildings on either side of the street were visible as they passed, though only partially, dark at the windows, with their doors shut tight. Most folks were where they ought to be, Sawyer supposed, gathered around stoves and fireplaces in their various homes, with coffee brewed and supper smells all around them.

Again, that bleak feeling of aloneness rose up inside him, but he quelled it quickly. He did not subscribe to melancholy moods —it wasn't the McKettrick way. In his family, a man—or a woman, for that matter— played the cards they were dealt, kept on going no matter what, and tended, to the best of their ability, to whatever task was presently at hand.

Still, there was a prickle at his nape, and Cherokee, rarely skittish, pranced sideways in agitation, tossing his head and neighing.

Sawyer had barely pushed back his long coat to uncover his Colt .45, just in case, when he heard the gunshot, swaddled in the snowy silence to a muted pop, saw the flash of orange fire and felt the bullet sear its way into his left shoulder. All of this transpired in the course of a second or so, but even as he slumped forward over Cherokee's neck, dazed by the hot-poker

thrust of the pain, spaces wedged themselves between moments, stretching time,
distorting it. Sawyer was at once a wounded
man, alone on a snow-blind street except
for his panicked horse, and a dispassion-
ate observer, nearby but oddly detached
from the scene.

He didn't see the shooter or his horse,
but the calm, watching part of him sized up
the situation, sensed there had been a rider.
If anybody had seen anything, or heard the
muffled gunshot, they weren't fixing to rush
to his rescue, and he didn't have the strength
to draw his .45, even if he could have seen
beyond Cherokee's laid-back ears.

Fortunately, the horse knew that—in
cases like this anyway—discretion was the
better part of valor. Cherokee bolted for
safer territory, leapfrogging through the
powdery snow, and Sawyer, hurting bad
and only half-conscious, simply lay over
the pommel, with the saddle horn jabbing
into his middle like a fist, and held on to
reins and mane for all he was worth.

Maybe the gunman lost sight of them in
the storm, or maybe he just slipped back
through the edges of Sawyer's awareness,
into the pulsing darkness that surrounded

him, but the second shot, the one that would have finished him off for sure, never came.

His mind slowed, and then slowed some more. He was aware of the *thud-thud-thud* of his heart, the raspy scratch of his breath, clawing its way into his lungs and then out again, and the familiar smell of wet horse-hide, but his vision dimmed to a gray haze.

Cherokee kept moving. Sawyer's consciousness seemed to retreat into the far corners of his mind, but growing up on the Triple M Ranch, in Arizona, he'd practically been raised on the back of a horse, and the muscles in his arms and legs must have drawn on some capacity for recollection beyond the grasp of the waking mind, because he managed to stay in the saddle.

It was only when the horse came to a sudden stop in a spill of buttery light on glistening snow that Sawyer pitched sideways with a sickening lurch, jarred his wounded shoulder when he struck the snow-padded ground, and passed out from the pain.

PIPER ST. JAMES, seated at the desk in her empty schoolroom and glumly surveying

the scrawny, undecorated pine tree leaning against the far wall, wished heartily,
and not for the first time, that she'd never
left Maine to strike out for a life of adven-
ture in the still-wild West.

Her cousin Dara Rose, in love with her
handsome rancher husband, had painted
a fine picture of Blue River in her letters,
telling Piper what a wonderful place it was,
full of good people and wide open to new-
comers.

Piper sighed. Of course Dara Rose
would see things that way—she was so
happy in her new marriage and, being a
generous soul, she wanted Piper to be
happy, too. Life had been hard for her
cousin and her two little girls, but Clay
McKettrick had changed all that.

Piper's pupils—all thirteen of them—
were safe at home, where they belonged,
and that was a considerable comfort to
her. She'd spent the entire day alone,
though, shut up in the schoolhouse, feeding the potbellied stove from an ever-
dwindling store of firewood, keeping herself
occupied as best she could. Tomorrow
was likely to bring more of the same, since

the storm showed no signs of letting up—it might even get worse.

Piper shuddered at the thought. She had plenty of food, thanks to the good people of Blue River, but her supply of well water was running out fast, like the wood. Soon, she'd have no choice but to pull on a pair of oversize boots, bundle up in both her everyday shawls *and* her heavy woolen cloak, raise the hood to protect her ears from the stinging chill, and slog her way across the schoolyard, once to the woodshed, and once to the well. To make matters worse, she was getting low on kerosene for the one lamp she'd allowed herself to light.

She told herself that Clay, Dara Rose's husband, would come by to check on her soon, but there was no telling when or if he'd be able to get there, given the distance and the state of the roads. For now, Piper had to do for herself.

The wind howled around the clapboard walls of that small, unpainted schoolhouse, sorrowful as a whole band of banshees searching for a way in, making her want to burrow under the quilts on her bed, which took up most of the tiny room in back set aside for teacher's quarters, and hide there until the weather turned.

She might freeze if she did that, of course, and that was if she didn't die of thirst beforehand.

So she put on the ungainly boots, left behind by Miss Krenshaw, the last teacher, wrapped herself in wool, drew a deep breath and opened the schoolhouse door to step out onto the little porch.

The cold buffeted her, hard as a slap, trapping the breath in her lungs and nearly knocking her backward, over the threshold.

Resolute, she drew the shawls and the cloak more tightly around her and tried again. The sooner she went out, the sooner she could come back *in,* she reasoned.

She stopped on the schoolhouse porch, peering through the goose-feather flakes coming down solid as a wall in front of her. Was that a horse, there in the thin light her one lamp cast through the front window?

Piper caught her breath, her heart thudding with sudden hope. There *was* a horse, and a horse meant a rider, and a rider meant company, if not practical help. Perhaps Clay *had* braved the tempest to pay her a visit—

She trudged down the steps and across the yard, every step an effort, and got a clearer look at the horse. A sturdy buckskin, the animal was real, all right. The creature was saddled, reins dangling, and she saw its eyes roll upward, glaring white.

But there was no rider on its back.

Although Piper had little experience with horses, she felt an instant affinity for the poor thing, evidently lost in the storm. It must have wandered off from somewhere nearby.

She moved toward it slowly, carefully, partly because of the bitter wind and partly because of her own rising trepidation. She didn't recognize the horse, which meant that Clay *hadn't* come to look in on her, nor had any of the other men—fathers, brothers or uncles of her students—who might have been concerned about the schoolmarm's welfare.

The buckskin whinnied wildly as she approached, backing up awkwardly, nearly falling onto its great, heaving haunches, lathered despite the chill.

"There, now," Piper said, reaching for the critter's bridle strap. There was a shed behind the schoolhouse—some of the students rode in from the country when class was in session and tethered their mounts there for the day, so there was some hay, and the plank walls offered a modicum of shelter—but just then, that shack seemed as far away as darkest Africa.

Before she could take hold of the horse's bridle, Piper tripped over something solid, half buried in the snow, fell to her hands and knees, and felt the sticky warmth of blood seeping through her mittens.

She saw him then, the rider, sprawled on his back, hat lying a few feet away, staining the snow to crimson.

Sitting on her haunches, Piper stared down at the unfortunate wayfarer for a few long moments, snowflakes slicing at her face like razors, confounded and afraid.

Bile surged into the back of her throat, scalding there, and she willed herself not to turn aside and retch. Something had to be done—and quickly.

"Mister?" she called, gripping the lapels of his long gunslinger's coat and bending close to his face. "Mister, are you alive?"

He groaned, and she saw one of his eyelids twitch.

The horse, close enough to step on one or both of them, whinnied again, a desperate sound.

"You'll be all right," Piper told both the horse and the man, on her knees in the snow, her mittens and cloak damp with blood, but she wasn't at all sure that was the truth.

The man was around six feet tall—there was no way she could lift him, and it was clear that he couldn't stand, let alone walk.

Piper deliberated briefly, then stumbled and struggled back into the schoolhouse, through to her room, and wrenched the patchwork quilt—she'd done the piecework herself and the task had been arduous—off the bed.

Warmer now, from the exertions of the past few minutes, Piper rushed outside again and somehow managed to get the quilt underneath the bleeding stranger. He opened his eyes once—even in the dim light she could see that they were a startling shade of greenish azure—and a little smile crooked the corner of his mouth before he passed into unconsciousness again.

In a frenzy of strength, she dragged man and quilt as far as the steps, but there was no getting him up them. She had no way of knowing how long he'd been lying in the schoolyard, injured, and frostbite was a serious possibility, as was hypothermia.

She gripped him by his shoulders—they were broad under her hands, and hard with muscle—and shook him firmly. "Mister!" she yelled, through the raging wind. "You've got to rally yourself enough to get up these steps—I can't do this without some assistance, and there's no one else around!"

Miraculously, the stranger came to and gathered enough strength to half crawl up the steps, with a lot of help from Piper. From there, she was able to pull him over the threshold onto the rough-plank floor, where he lay facedown, bleeding copiously and only semiconscious.

"My horse," he rasped.

"Bother your horse," Piper replied, but she didn't mean it. The stranger, being a human being, was her first concern, but she was almost as worried about that frightened animal standing outside in the weather, and she knew she wouldn't be able to ignore it.

"Horse," the man repeated.

"I'll see to him," Piper promised, having no real choice in the matter. She collected another blanket from her quarters, covered the man, and steeled herself to hurry back outside.

Ever after, she'd wonder how she'd managed such an impossible feat, but at the time, Piper worked from a sense of expediency. She got hold the horse's reins and somehow led him around back, through what seemed like miles of snow, and into the dark shed. There, she removed his saddle, the blanket beneath it, and the bridle. She spread out some hay for him and found a bucket, which she filled with snow—that being the best she could do for now. When the snow melted, the creature would have drinking water.

The horse was jumpy at first, and Piper took a few precious moments to speak softly to him, rubbing him down as best she could with an old burlap sack and making the same promise as before—he *would* be all right, and so would his master, because she wouldn't have it any other way.

On the way back to the schoolhouse, she fought her way into the woodshed and filled her arms with sticks of pitch-scented pine.

The stranger was still on the floor, upon her return, lying just over the threshold, either dead or sleeping.

Hastily, murmuring a prayer under her breath, Piper dumped the firewood into the box beside the stove, went back to the man, pulled off one ruined mitten and felt for a pulse at the base of his throat. His skin was cold, a shade of grayish-blue, but there was a heartbeat, thank heaven, faint but steady.

There was still water to fetch—why hadn't she done this chore earlier, in the daylight, as she'd intended, instead of starting a pot of pinto beans and reading one of Sir Walter Scott's novels?—and Piper didn't allow herself to think beyond getting to the well, filling a couple of buckets, and bringing them inside.

She marched outside again, moving like a woman floundering in a bad dream, taking the water buckets with her. Just getting to the well took most of her strength and, once there, she had to lower the vessels, one by one, by a length of rope.

She'd discarded her mittens by then, and the rough hemp burned like fire against her palms and the undersides of her fingers, but she lowered and filled one bucket, and then the other. Her hands ached ferociously as she carried those heavy pails toward the schoolhouse, up the steps, and once inside, she set them both down an instant before she would surely have spilled them all over the man lying in a swoon on her floor.

There was no time to spare—if there had been, Piper might have had the luxury of succumbing to helplessness and giving herself up to a fit of useless weeping—so she filled a kettle and put it on the stove to heat, right next to the simmering beans.

With one eye on the inert visitor the whole time, she peeled off her bloody cloak and shawls and stepped out of the boots. Her hands were numb, and she shook them hard, hoping to restore the circulation, which only made them hurt again. When the water was warm enough, she

poured some into a basin and scrubbed
sticky streaks of crimson from her skin.

The stranger didn't stir, even once, and
he might very well be dead, but Piper talked
to him anyway, in the same brisk, take-
charge tone she used when her students
balked at staying behind their desks, where
they belonged. "You can stop fretting over
your horse," she said. "He's safe in the
shed, with hay and water aplenty."

There was no response, and Piper
made herself walk over to the man, stoop,
and, once again, feel for a pulse.

It was there, and it seemed the bleeding
had slowed, if not stopped altogether.

She was thankful for small favors.

Noticing the ominous-looking gun jut-
ting from a holster on his right hip, she
shivered, extracted the thing gingerly, by
two fingers. It was heavy, and the handle
was intricately carved, as well as blood-
speckled. She made out the initials *S.M.*
as she held the dreadful weapon in shak-
ing hands, carried it into the cloakroom
and set it carefully on a high shelf.

Heat surged audibly into the water kettle, causing it to rattle cheerfully on the
stovetop. Piper moved, with quiet diligence,

from one effort to another, emptying the basin in which she'd washed her hands through a wide crack in the floorboards, wiping it out with a rag, settling it aside. She had cloth strips to use as bandages, since one or the other of her pupils were always getting hurt during recess, and there was a bottle of iodine, too, so she fetched these from their customary places in the cabinet behind her desk.

Her mind kept going back to that dreadful pistol. No one carried guns these days—it was the twentieth century, after all—except for lawmen, like Clay, who was the marshal of Blue River, and, well, *outlaws*.

Had the stranger used that long-barreled weapon to hold up banks, rob trains, accost law-abiding citizens on the road? She'd seen no sign of a badge, so he probably wasn't a constable of any sort, but he might have identification of some kind, in his pockets, perhaps, or the saddlebags, left behind in the shed with the horse and its attendant gear.

Put it out of your mind, she ordered herself. There was no sense in pandering to her imagination.

Since she couldn't quite face searching the fellow's pockets—it seemed too
intimate an undertaking—she turned her
thoughts to other things. After collecting a
pair of scissors from the drawer of her battered oak desk, Piper undertook the task
she would rather have avoided, kneeling
beside the man's prone form and gently
rolling him onto his back.

The singular odors of gunpowder and
blood rose like smoke, one acrid, one me-
tallic, to fill her nostrils, then her lungs, then
her fretful stomach. She gagged again,
swallowed hard, and forced her trembling
hands to pick up the scissors and begin
snipping away at the front of the man's
once-fine coat.

The bullet had torn its way through the
dark, costly fabric, through the shirt—
probably white once—and the flesh beneath.

When Piper finally uncovered the
wound, she was horrified all over again.
She slapped one hand over her mouth,
though whether to hold back a scream or
a spate of sickness she couldn't have said.

The deep, jagged hole in the flesh of the
stranger's shoulder began to seep again.

Piper shifted her gaze to the supplies she'd gathered, now resting beside her on the floor—a basin full of steaming water, strands of clean cloth, iodine—and was struck by their inadequacy, and her own.

This man needed a surgeon, not the bumbling first aid of a schoolmarm.

She raised her eyes to the night-darkened window and the huge flakes of falling snow beyond, and mentally calculated the distance to Dr. Howard's house, on the far side of Blue River.

At most a ten-minute walk away, in daylight and decent weather, Doc's place might as well have been on another continent, for all the chance she had of reaching it safely. Furthermore, the man wasn't a physician, but a dentist, albeit a very competent one who would definitely know what do to in such an emergency.

Since she had no means of summoning him, she would have to do what she could, and hope the Good Lord would lend a hand.

Piper spent the next half hour or so cleaning that wound, treating it with iodine, binding it closed with the strips of cloth. Stitches were needed, she knew, but

threading a needle and sewing flesh together, the way she might stitch up a
patchwork quilt, was entirely beyond her. If
she made the attempt, she'd get sick, faint
dead away, or both, thereby making bad
matters considerably worse.

Mercifully, the stranger did not wake
during the long, careful process of apply-
ing the bandages. When she'd finished,
Piper covered him again, brought a pillow
and eased it under his head, and, rising to
her feet, looked down at the front of her
dress.

Like the cloak and the mittens, it was
badly stained.

Piper rinsed the basin, filled it with clean
water, and retreated into the little room at
the back of the schoolhouse. She stripped
to her petticoat and camisole, shivering all
the while, and gave herself a quick sponge
bath. After that, she donned a calico
dress—a little scant for the season, but
she'd need her gray woolen one for some
time yet and wanted to keep it clean. Once
properly clad again, she took her dark hair
down from its pins and combs, brushed it
vigorously, and secured it into a loose chignon at her nape.

Needing to keep herself occupied, Piper burned her knitted mittens in the stove—there was no use trying to get them clean—and then assessed the damage to her cloak. It was dire.

Resigned, and keeping one eye on the unmoving victim, Piper took up her scissors again and cut away the stained parts of her only cloak, consigned the pieces to the stove, and folded what remained to be used for other purposes.

Waste not, want not. She and Dara Rose, growing up together in a household of genteel poverty, had learned that lesson early and well.

She ate supper at her desk—a bowl of the beans she'd been simmering on the stove all afternoon—and wondered what to do next.

She was exhausted, and every muscle ached from the strain of dragging a full-grown man halfway across the schoolyard and inside, tending to the horse as well as its master, fetching the wood and the water. She didn't dare close her eyes to sleep, though—the stranger might be incapacitated, but he was *still* a stranger, and he was accustomed to carrying a

gun. Suppose he came to and did—well—
something?

From a safe distance, Piper assessed
him again, cataloging his features in her
mind. Caramel-colored hair, a lean, muscular frame, expensive clothes and boots.
And then there was the horse, obviously
a sturdy creature, well-bred. This man
was probably a person of means, she
concluded, but that certainly didn't mean
he wasn't a rascal and a rounder, too.

He might actually be dangerous, a drifter
or an unscrupulous opportunist.

Again, she considered braving the
weather once more, making her way to the
nearest house to ask for help, since Doc's
place was too distant, but she knew she'd
never make it even that far. She had no
cloak, and in that blizzard, she didn't dare
trust her sense of direction. She might
head the wrong way, wander off into the
countryside somewhere and perish from
exposure.

She shuddered again, rose from her
chair, and carried her empty bowl and
soup spoon back to the washstand in her
quarters, where she left them to be dealt
with later.

Still giving the stranger a fairly wide berth, she perched on one of the students' benches and watched him, thinking hard. She supposed she could peel that overcoat off him, put it on, and tramp to the neighbors' house, nearly a quarter of a mile away, but the effort might do him further injury and, besides, the mere thought of wearing that bloody garment made her ill.

Even if she'd been able to bear *that*, the problem of the weather remained.

She was stuck.

She retrieved her knitting—a scarf she'd intended to give to Dara Rose as a Christmas gift—and sat working stitches and waiting for the man to move, or speak.

Or die.

"Water," he said, after a long time. "I need—water."

New energy rushed through Piper's small body; she filled a ladle from one of the buckets she'd hauled in earlier, carried it carefully to his side, and knelt to slip one hand under his head and raise him up high enough to drink.

He took a few sips and his eyes searched

her face as she lowered him back to the floor.

"Where—? Who—?" he muttered, the words as rough as sandpaper.

"You're in the Blue River schoolhouse," she answered. "I'm Miss St. James, the teacher. Who are you?"

"Is . . . my horse—?"

Piper managed a thin smile. She didn't know whether to be glad because he'd regained consciousness or worried by the problems that might present. "Your horse is fine. In out of the storm, fed and watered."

A corner of his mouth quirked upward, ever so slightly, and his eyes seemed clearer than when he'd opened them before, as though he were more present somehow, and centered squarely within the confines of his own skin and bones. "That's . . . good," he said, with effort.

"Who are you?" Piper asked. She still hadn't searched his pockets, since just binding up his wound had taken all the courage and fortitude she could muster.

He didn't answer, but gestured for more water, lifting his head without her help this time, and when he'd swallowed most of the ladle's contents, he lapsed into another faint. His skin was ghastly pale, and his lips had a bluish tinge.

He belonged in a bed, not on the floor, but moving him any farther was out of the question, given their difference in size. All she could do was cover him, keep the fire going—and pray for a miraculous recovery.

The night passed slowly, with the man groaning hoarsely in his sleep now and then, and muttering a woman's name— Josie—often. At times, he seemed almost desperate for a response.

Oddly stricken by these murmured cries, Piper left her chair several times to kneel beside him, holding his hand.

"I'm here," she'd say, hoping he'd think she was this Josie person.

Whoever she was.

He'd smile in his sleep then, and rest peacefully for a while, and Piper would go back to her chair and her knitting. At some point, she unraveled the scarf and cast on new stitches; she'd make mittens instead, she decided, to replace the ones she'd had to burn. With so much of the winter still to come, she'd need them, and heaven only knew what she'd do for a cloak; since her salary was barely enough to keep body and soul together. Such a purchase was close to impossible.

She wasn't normally the fretful sort—like Dara Rose, she was hardworking and practical and used to squeezing pennies—but, then, this was hardly a normal situation.

Was this man an outlaw? Perhaps even a murderer?

He was well dressed and he owned a horse of obvious quality, even to her untrained eyes, but, then, maybe he was highly skilled at thievery, and his belongings were ill-gotten gains.

Piper nodded off in her chair, awakened with a start, saw that it was morning and the snow had relented a little, still heavy but no longer an impenetrable curtain of white.

The stranger was either asleep or unconscious, and the thin sunlight struck his toast-colored hair with glints of gold.

He was handsome, Piper decided. All the more reason to keep her distance.

She set aside her knitting and proceeded

to build up the fire and then put a pot of coffee on to brew, hoping the stuff would restore her waning strength, and finally wrapped herself in her two remaining shawls, drew a deep breath, and left the schoolhouse to trudge around back, to the shed.

The trees were starkly beautiful, every branch defined, as if etched in glimmering frost.

To her relief, the buckskin was fine, though the water bucket she'd filled with snow was empty.

Piper patted the horse, picked up the bucket, and made her way back to the well to fill it. When she got back, the big gelding greeted her with a friendly nicker and drank thirstily from the pail.

As she was returning to the shelter of the schoolhouse, holding her skirts up so she wouldn't trip over the hem, she spotted a rider just approaching the gate at the top of the road and recognized him immediately, even through the falling snow.

Clay McKettrick.

Piper's whole being swelled with relief.

She waited, saw Clay's grin flash from beneath the round brim of his hat. His horse high-stepped toward her, across the field of snow, steam puffing from its flared nostrils, its mane and tail spangled with tiny icicles.

"I told Dara Rose you'd be fine here on your own," Clay remarked cordially, dismounting a few feet from where Piper stood, all but overwhelmed with gratitude, "but she insisted on finding out for sure." A pause, a troubled frown as he took in her rumpled calico dress. "Where's your coat? You'll catch your death traipsing around without it."

She ignored the question, wide-eyed and winded from the hard march through the snow.

Clay was a tall, lean man, muscular in all the right places, and it wasn't hard to see why her cousin loved him so much. He was pleasing to look at, certainly, but his best feature, in Piper's opinion, was his rock-solid character. He exuded quiet strength and confidence in all situations.

He would know what to do in this crisis, and he would *do* it.

"There's a man inside," Piper blurted, finding her voice at last and gesturing toward the schoolhouse. By then, the cold was indeed penetrating her thin dress. "He's been shot. His horse is in the shed and—"

Clay's expression turned serious, and he brushed past her, leaving his own mount to stand patiently in the yard.

Piper hurried into the schoolhouse behind Clay.

He crouched, laying one hand to the man's unhurt shoulder. "Sawyer?" he rasped. "Damn it, Sawyer—*what happened to you*?"

CHAPTER 2

Sawyer, Piper thought distractedly—
Sawyer *McKettrick*, Clay's cousin, the man
he'd been expecting for weeks now. That
explained the initials on the man's holster,
if not much else.

Down on one knee beside the other
man now, Clay took off his snowy hat and
tossed it aside. Piper caught the glint of
his nickel-plated badge, a star pinned to
the front of his heavy coat. Clay was still
Blue River's town marshal, but it was a job
he was ready to hand over to someone
else, so he could concentrate on ranching
and his growing family.

"Sawyer!" Clay repeated, his tone brusque with concern.

Sawyer's eyes rolled open, and a grin played briefly on his mouth. "I must have died and gone to hell," he said in a slow, raspy drawl, "because I'd swear I've come face-to-face with the devil himself."

Clay gave a raucous chuckle at that. "You must be better off than you look," he commented. "Can you get to your feet?"

Solemnly amused, Sawyer considered the question for a few moments, moistened his lips, which were dry and cracked despite Piper's repeated efforts to give him water during the night, and struggled to reply, "I don't think so."

"That's all right," Clay said, gruffly gentle, while Piper's weary mind raced. She'd heard a few things about Sawyer, and some of it was worrisome—for instance, no one, including Clay, seemed to know which side of the law he was on—though Dara Rose had liked him. "I'll help you." With that, Clay raised Sawyer to a sitting position, causing him to moan again and his bandages to seep with patches of bright red, draped his cousin's good arm over his shoulders, and stood, bringing the other man up with him.

"I'll put Sawyer on your bed, if that's all right," Clay said to Piper, already headed toward her quarters in the back. The schoolhouse was small, and everybody knew how it was laid out, since the building of it had been a community effort.

When word got around that she'd harbored a man under this roof, bleeding and insensible with pain or not, her reputation would be tarnished, at best.

At worst? Completely ruined.

The injustice of that was galling to Piper, but nonetheless binding. Lady teachers in particular were scrutinized for the slightest inclination toward wanton behavior, though their male counterparts sometimes courted and then married one of their students, with impunity. A practice Piper considered reprehensible.

"Certainly," she said now, well aware that Clay hadn't been asking her permission but feeling compelled to offer some kind of response.

She hovered in the doorway of her

room—little more than a lean-to, really—
with one tiny window, high up, while Clay
wrestled Sawyer out of his coat then eased
him down carefully onto the bed, pulled off
his boots.

The effort of going even that far must
have been too much for Sawyer, strong as
he looked, because he shut his eyes again,
and didn't respond when Clay spoke to
him.

"I'll get the doc," Clay said to Piper, as
she stepped out of the doorway to let him
pass. "Do you have any more blankets?
It's important to keep him warm."

Piper thought with a heavy heart of the
fine, colorful quilts lying neatly folded in
her hope chest. She'd always envisioned
them gracing the beds of some lovely
house, once she was married, like Dara
Rose, with a proper home.

"Yes," she said bravely, and though she
didn't begrudge Sawyer McKettrick those
quilts, she couldn't help lamenting their
fate. She'd worked hard to assemble them
from tiny scraps of fabric, carefully saved,
and many of the pieces were all she had
to remember friends she'd left behind in
Maine.

She swept over to her bulky cedar chest, raised the lid, and rummaged through the treasured contents—doilies and potholders, tablecloths and dish towels and the like—until she'd found what she was looking for.

As she spread the first of those exquisitely stitched coverlets over Mr. McKettrick, he stirred again, opened his eyes briefly, and smiled. "Thanks, Josie," he said, and there was a caress in the way he said the name.

Briskly, because she was a little hurt, though she couldn't have pinpointed the reason why such an emotion should afflict her, Piper put another quilt on top of her patient, and then another.

Then, because it was nearly eight o'clock, she went to the other end of the building, where the bell rope dangled, and gave it a tug. Surely none of her pupils would make it to school on such a day, but Piper believed in maintaining routine, especially during trying times. There was something reassuring about it.

The silvery bell, high overhead in its little belfry, chimed once, twice, three times, summoning students who would not come.

Piper's hands, rope-burned from hauling up well water the night before, stung fiercely, and she was almost glad, because the pain gave her something to think about besides the man sprawled on her spinster's bed, probably bleeding all over her quilts.

She retrieved a tin of Wildflower Salve from her bureau, careful not to make too much noise and disturb Mr. McKettrick. Carrying the salve back to her schoolroom, she sat down at her desk and smiled a little as she twisted off the pretty little lid to treat her sore palms.

There was an abundance of the stuff, since Dara Rose, impoverished after the scandalous death of her first husband, upstairs at the Bitter Gulch Saloon, had once planned to sell the product door-to-door in hopes of making enough money to support herself and her two small daughters, Edrina and Harriet. Instead, Dara Rose had fallen in love with Clay McKettrick, married him, and thus retained what amounted to a lifetime supply of medicinal salve, which she generously shared.

A half hour passed before Clay returned,

with Dr. Jim Howard, the local dentist, riding stalwartly along beside him on the mule that usually pulled his buggy.

Everybody in Blue River liked Dr. Howard, whose young daughter, Madeline, was one of Piper's best students. At eight, the little girl could read and cipher with the acuity of an adult. *Mrs.* Howard, however, was not so easy to like as her husband and daughter. Eloise wore nothing but velvet or silk, dismissed the town as a "bump in the road" and told anyone who would listen that she'd "married down."

"Miss St. James," Dr. Howard greeted her, with a friendly smile and a tug at the brim of his Eastern-style hat, as he stomped the snow off his boots on the schoolhouse porch, the way Clay had done a moment before. Doc was a large man, good-natured, older than his wife by some twenty years, and his eyes were a kindly shade of blue. He carried a battered leather bag in one gloved hand.

Piper barely stopped herself from rushing over and embracing the man, she was so glad to see him. The responsibility of keeping Mr. McKettrick alive had, she realized, weighed more heavily upon her than she'd thought it did.

She merely nodded in acknowledgment, though, as he closed the door against the cold daylight wind, and she hung back when Clay led the way through the schoolroom and into the chamber behind it.

Of course she couldn't help overhearing most of the conversation between Clay and Dr. Howard, given that the whole place was hardly larger than Dara Rose's chicken coop out on the ranch, classroom, teacher's quarters and all.

Clay was asking how bad the injury was, and Dr. Howard replied that it was serious enough, but with luck and a lot of rest, the patient would probably recover.

Probably recover? Piper thought, sipping from the mug of coffee she'd poured for herself. When Clay and the doctor—more commonly referred to as "Doc"—came out of the back room, she'd offer them some, too. She owned three cups, not including the bone china tea service for six nestled in her hope chest, which would remain precisely where it was, unlike her once pristine quilts.

"I'd like to take Sawyer out to my place," she heard Clay say.

"Better wait a few days," came Doc's response. "He's lost a lot of blood. The bullet went clear through him, though, which saves me having to dig it out, and Miss St. James did a creditable job of binding him up. He'll have scars, but the wound looks clean, thanks to her." A pause followed. "There's a bottle of carbolic acid in my bag there—hand it to me, will you?"

There was another short silence, during which Clay must have done as Doc asked, soon followed by a hoarse shout of angry protest from the patient. He swore colorfully, and Piper winced. She believed that cursing revealed a poor vocabulary, among other personal shortcomings.

"Can't take a chance on infection setting in," the dentist said peaceably, evidently unruffled by the outburst. "The burning will stop after a while."

Sawyer muttered something unintelligible.

Piper's hands trembled as she set her coffee mug down on her desk. Doc's reply to Clay's statement about taking his cousin out to the ranch echoed in her mind. *Better wait a few days.*

All well and good, she thought fretfully, but what was *she* supposed to do in the meantime? There was only one bed, after all, and she couldn't sleep in a chair until the man was well enough to be moved, could she?

Mr. McKettrick was indeed badly injured, but this was a *schoolhouse*, frequented by children five days a week—children who would go home after dismissal and tell their parents there was a strange man recuperating in Miss St. James's room. She wouldn't be able to hide him from them any more than she could hide that enormous gelding of his, quartered in the shed out back. Even unconscious, Sawyer filled the place with his presence, breathed up all the air.

Clay emerged from her room just then, took a second mug from the shelf near the stove and poured himself some coffee. He was probably cold, Piper realized with some chagrin, having ridden in from the ranch, proceeded to Doc Howard's, and then made his way back to the schoolhouse again.

"I guess we've got a problem," he said now. Was there a twinkle in those very blue eyes of his as he studied her expression?

"Yes," Piper agreed, somewhat stiffly. Maybe Clay found the situation amusing, but *she* certainly didn't.

Clay took another sip, thoughtful and slow, from his mug. He'd shed his long coat soon after he and Doc arrived, and his collarless shirt was open at the throat, showing the ridged fabric of his undergarment. Like Sawyer, he wore a gun belt, but he'd set the pistol aside earlier, an indication of his good manners. "You probably heard what Doc Howard said," he told her, after a few moments of pensive consideration. "I could stay here with Sawyer and send you on out to the ranch to stay with Dara Rose and the girls, but it's hard going, with the snow still so deep."

Jim Howard came out of Piper's room, wiping his hands clean on a cloth that smelled of carbolic acid. "I gave him some laudanum," he told Clay. "He'll sleep for a while."

Piper propped her own hands on her hips. She'd spent a mostly sleepless night hoping and praying that someone would come to help, and she'd gotten her wish, but for all that, the problem was only partially solved.

Perhaps she should have been more specific, she reflected, rueful.

"Must I point out to you gentlemen," she began, with dignity, "that this arrangement is highly improper?"

Clay's grin was slight, but it was, nonetheless, a grin, and it infuriated her. She was an unmarried woman, a schoolmarm, and there was *a man in her bed,* likely to remain there for the foreseeable future. All her dreams for the future—a good husband, a home, and children of her own— could be compromised, and through no fault of her own.

"I understand your dilemma, Piper," he said, sounding like an indulgent older brother, "but you heard the doc. Sawyer can't be moved until that wound of his mends a little."

"Surely you could take him as far as the hotel without doing harm," Piper reasoned, quietly frantic. She kept her hands at her sides, but the urge to wring them was strong.

Dr. Howard shook his head. Helped himself to the last mug and some coffee. "That could kill him," he said bluntly, but his expression was sympathetic. "I'm sure Eloise wouldn't mind coming over and helping with his care, though. She's had some nursing experience, and it would temper any gossip that might arise."

As far as Piper was concerned, being shut up with Eloise Howard for any length of time would be worse than attending to the needs of a helpless stranger by herself. *Much* worse.

"I couldn't ask her to do that," Piper said quickly. "Mrs. Howard has you and little Madeline to look after." She turned a mild glare on Clay. "Your cousin needs *male* assistance," she added. She'd dragged Sawyer McKettrick in out of the cold, cleaned his wound, even taken care of his horse, but she wasn't *about* to help him use the chamber pot, and that was final.

"I'll do what I can," Clay said, "but Dara Rose is due to have our baby any day now. I can't leave her out there alone, with just the girls and a few ranch hands. Once the weather lets up, though . . ."

His words fell away as Piper's cheeks

flared with the heat of frustration. She could demand to be put up in the hotel herself, of course, until Sawyer McKettrick was well enough to leave the schoolhouse, but that would mean he'd be alone here. And he was in serious condition, despite Doc's cheerful prognosis.

What if something went wrong?

Besides, staying in hotels cost money, and even there in the untamed West, many of them had policies against admitting single women—unless, of course, they were ladies of the evening, and thus permitted to slip in through an alley door, under cover of darkness, and climb the back stairs to ply their wretched trade.

"You do realize," Piper persisted, "that I have nowhere to sleep?" *And no good man will* ever *marry me because my morals will forever be in question, even though I've done nothing wrong.*

Dr. Howard walked over and laid a fatherly hand on her shoulder. "I'll bring over anything you need," he assured her. "And stop in as often as I can. I'm sure Clay will do the same."

Clay nodded, but he was looking out the window, at the ceaseless snow, and his expression was troubled. "I've got to get back to Dara Rose," he said.

Piper's heart went out to him. As untenable as *her* situation was, Dara Rose needed Clay right now, and so did the children. Edrina and Harriet, though uncommonly precocious, were still quite small, and they couldn't be expected to know what to do if their mother went into labor.

"Go home, Clay," she said gently. "Give Dara Rose my best regards. Edrina and Harriet, too."

Clay's expression was even more serious now, and he looked at her for a long time before giving a reluctant nod and promising, "I'll come back for Sawyer as soon as Doc decides he can travel. I appreciate this, Piper. I wouldn't ask it of you, but—"

"I understand," she said, when words failed him again. And she *did* understand. Clay and Sawyer, like Piper and Dara Rose, were first cousins, the next best thing to siblings, and the bond was strong between them.

The snow came down harder and then harder still, and Doc Howard finished his coffee, collected his bag and took one more look at Sawyer, then headed out, after assuring Piper that he'd return before day's end and asking what he ought to bring back.

Blankets, she'd said, flustered, and kerosene, and whatever medicine the patient might need.

Clay attended to Sawyer's horse, said goodbye, and left for the ranch.

Watching him disappear into a spinning vortex of white, Piper felt a lump rise in her throat.

Once again, she was alone, except for Sawyer McKettrick and he, of course, was a hindrance, not a help.

True to his word, Doc was back within the hour, despite the increasingly bad weather, bringing a fresh supply of laudanum, a jug of kerosene, more carbolic acid and several warm blankets, wrapped in oilcloth so they'd stay dry.

He examined Sawyer again—reporting that he was still sleeping but that his heartbeat was stronger than before and he seemed to be breathing more easily—gave Piper a few instructions, and quickly left again, because nightfall would be coming on soon, making the ordinarily short journey home even more difficult than it already was.

Piper thanked him, asked him to give Eloise and Madeline her best, and watched through the front window until he and his mule were gone from sight.

Then, feeling more alone than she ever had, she got busy.

She washed down the already clean blackboard.

She dusted every surface in the schoolroom and refilled the kerosene lamp.

She drank more coffee and fed more wood into the stove.

Before he'd gone, Clay had assured her that Sawyer's horse would be fine until morning, which meant she could stay inside, where it was comparatively warm, so that was *one* less worry, anyhow. Gaps between the floorboards let in some of the cold, but that couldn't be helped. Using the spare blankets Doc had brought, she made a bed on the floor, close to the stove and hoped all the mice were hibernating.

She lit the kerosene lamp as the room darkened, and tried to cheer herself up by imagining the Christmas tree, still in its pail of water and leaning against the far wall, glowing with bright decorations. She took comfort in its green branches and faintly piney scent and thought, with a smile, of the recitations her students were memorizing for the school program.

Christmas Eve, just ten days away, fell on a Friday that year, so school would be in session until noon—weather permitting— and the recital would be presented soon after. After the poems and skits, everyone would sing carols. The owner of the mercantile had promised to donate oranges and peppermint sticks for the children, and the parents would bring pies and cookies and cakes.

This gathering represented all the Christmas some of the children would have, and all thirteen of them were looking forward to the celebration.

She moved, quiet as a wraith, to the window, and glumness settled over her spirit as she looked out.

And still the snow fell in abundance, unrelenting.

IT WAS THE pain that finally roused him.

Sawyer came to the surface of consciousness with a fierce jolt, feeling as though he'd been speared through his left shoulder.

His stomach lurched, and for a moment he was out there on that snowy street again, unable to see his assailant, reaching in vain for his .45.

He went deliberately still—not only was there no Colt at his hip, but he'd been stripped to his birthday suit—and tried to orient himself to reality.

The room was dark and a little chilly, and it smelled faintly of some flowery cologne, which probably meant there was a woman around somewhere.

The thought made him smile, despite the lingering pain, which had transmuted itself from a stabbing sensation to a burning ache in the few minutes since he'd opened his eyes. There weren't many situations that couldn't be improved by the presence of a lady.

He squinted, managed to raise himself a little, with the pillows behind him providing support. Snow-speckled moonlight entered through the one window, set high in the wall, and spilled onto the intricate patterns of the several quilts that covered him to the waist.

"Hullo?" he called into the darkness.

She appeared in the doorway then, carrying a flickering kerosene lamp, a small but well-made woman with dark hair and a wary way of carrying herself.

She looked familiar, but Sawyer couldn't quite place her.

"You're awake, then," she said rhetorically, staying well away from the bed, as if she thought he might grab hold of her. The impression left him vaguely indignant. "Are you hungry?"

"No," he said, because his stomach, though empty, was still reacting to the rush of pain that had awakened him. "How's my horse?"

In the light of the lantern, he saw her smile slightly. Decided she was pretty, if a mite on the scrawny side. Her waist looked no bigger around than a fence post, and she wasn't very tall, either.

"Your horse is quite comfortable," she said. "Are you in pain? The doctor left laudanum in case you needed it."

Sawyer guessed, from the bitter taste in his mouth, that he'd already had at least one dose, and he was reluctant to take another. Basically distilled opium, the stuff caused horrendous nightmares and fogged up his brain.

"I'm all right," he said.

She didn't move.

He had fuzzy memories of being shot and falling off his horse, but he wasn't sure if he'd actually seen his cousin Clay or just dreamed he was there. He did recollect the doctor, though—that sawbones had poured liquid fire into the gaping hole in his shoulder, made him yell because it hurt so bad.

"Do you have a name?" he asked.

She bristled, and he guessed at the color of her eyes—dark blue, maybe, or brown. It was hard to tell, in the glare of that lantern she was holding. "Of course I do," she replied primly. "Do you?"

Sawyer gave a raw chuckle at that. She was an impertinent little dickens, he thought, probably able to hold her own in an argument. "Sawyer McKettrick," he conceded, with a slight nod of his head. "I'm Clay's cousin, here to take over as town marshal."

"Well," she said, remaining in the

doorway, "you're off to a wonderful start, aren't you?"

He chuckled again, though it took more energy than he felt he could spare. "Yes, ma'am," he said. "I reckon I am."

"Piper St. James," she said then, without laying any groundwork beforehand.

"What?"

"You asked for my name." A pause, during which she raised the lantern a little higher, saw that he was bare-chested, and quickly lowered it again. "You can call me 'Miss James.'"

"Thanks for that, anyhow," he said, enjoying the exchange, however feeble it was on his end. "Thanks for looking after my horse, too, and, unless I miss my guess, saving my life."

Miss St. James's spine lengthened; she must have been all of five foot two, and probably weighed less than his saddlebags. "I couldn't just leave you lying out there in the snow," she said, with a sort of puckish modesty.

From her tone, Sawyer concluded that she'd considered doing just that, though, fortunately for him, her conscience must have overruled the idea.

"You'd have had to step over me every time you went out," he teased, "and that would have been awkward."

He thought she smiled then, though he couldn't be sure because the light fell forward from the lantern and left her mostly in shadow.

"What is this place?" he asked presently, when she didn't speak.

"You're in the Blue River schoolhouse," Miss St. James informed him. "I teach here."

"I see," Sawyer said, wearying, though he was almost as much in the dark, literally and figuratively, as before he'd asked the question. "Was Clay here?" he threw out. "Or did I imagine that part?"

"He was here," Miss St. James confirmed. "He's gone home now—his wife is expecting a baby soon, and he didn't like leaving her alone—but he'll be back as soon as the weather allows."

Sawyer was quiet for a while, gathering scraps of strength, trying to breathe his way past a sudden swell of pain. "You don't have to be scared of me," he told her, after a long time.

"I'm not," she lied, still cautious. Still keeping her distance.

"I reckon I can't blame you," Sawyer said, closing his eyes to regain his equilibrium. The pain rose to a new crescendo, and the room had begun to pitch and sway.

"The laudanum is there on the nightstand," she informed him helpfully, evidently seeing more than he'd wanted her to. "And the chamber pot is under the bed."

He felt his lips twitch. "I'll keep that in mind," he said.

"You're certain you don't want something to eat?"

"Maybe later," he managed to reply.

He thought she'd go away then, but she hesitated. "You were asking for someone named Josie," she said. "Perhaps when the weather is better, we could send word to her, that you've been hurt, I mean."

Sawyer opened his eyes again, swiftly enough to set the little room to spinning again. "That won't be necessary," he bit out, but he felt a certain bitter amusement imagining what would happen if word of his misfortune were to reach her. Josie was his last employer's very fetching wife, and she'd made it clear that she wanted more from Sawyer than protection and cordial conversation. He'd had the same problem before, with other wives of men he worked for, along with their sisters and daughters in some instances, and he'd always managed to sidestep any romantic entanglements, be they physical or emotional—until Josie.

He'd *wanted* Josie, and that was why he'd agreed to come to Blue River and fill in for Clay, as temporary marshal—to put some distance between himself and the sweet temptation to bed his boss's wife, to burn in her fire, let lust consume him.

He'd left in the nick of time.

Or had he?

Had the shooter been one of Henry Vandenburg's hirelings, one of his own former colleagues, sent to make sure Sawyer stayed away from the old man's wife—forever?

It was possible, of course. Vandenburg was rich, and he was powerful, and he probably wasn't above having a rival dispensed with, but even for him, ordering the murder of one of Angus McKettrick's grandsons would have been pretty risky. His and Clay's granddad, even at his advanced age, was a force of nature in his own right, owning half of Arizona as he did, and so were his four sons. Holt, Rafe, Kade—Sawyer's father—and Jeb, who'd sired Clay, were all law-abiding citizens, happily married men with children and even a few grandchildren, money in the bank and a prosperous ranch to run. Still, the untimely death of any member of the clan would rouse them to Earp-like fury, and Vandenburg surely knew that. In fact, it was that dogged quality that had caused the old reprobate to hire Sawyer as a bodyguard in the first place.

"Mr. McKettrick?" Miss Piper St. James was standing right beside the bed now, holding the lantern high. There was concern in her voice—enough to draw her to his bedside, thereby risking some nefarious assault on her virtue. "Are you all right? For a moment, you looked—I thought . . ."

She lapsed awkwardly into silence.

He might have reminded her, if he'd had the strength, that, *no*, actually, he *wasn't* "all right," because he'd been *shot*. Instead, he asked slowly, measuring out each word like a storekeeper dispensing sugar or flour, "Do you happen to have any whiskey on hand?"

CHAPTER 3

"Of course I don't have any whiskey," Piper replied, with a little more sharpness in her tone than she'd intended to exercise. "This is a *school,* not a roadhouse."

"Well, damn," Sawyer said, affably gruff and clearly still in pain. "I could sure use a shot of good old-fashioned rotgut right about now. Might take the edge off."

Having set the kerosene lantern on the nightstand so she wouldn't drop it and set the whole place on fire, Piper took a step back. Rotgut, indeed. "Then I guess it's too bad you fell off your horse here instead of in front of the Bitter Gulch Saloon."

He favored her with a squinty frown at this, and she wondered distractedly what he'd look like in the daylight, cleaned up and wearing something besides bandages, her quilts and the dish-towel sling Dr. Howard had put on his left arm. "Are you one of those hatchet-swinging types?" he asked, with a note of benign disapproval. "The kind who go around hacking perfectly good bars to splinters, shattering mirrors and breaking every bottle on the shelves?"

Piper stiffened slightly, offended, though she couldn't think why she ought to give a pin about this man's—this *stranger's*—opinion of her. "No," she said tersely. "If some people choose to pollute their systems with poison, to the detriment of their wives and children and society in general, it's none of my concern."

He laughed then, a hoarse bark of a sound, brittle with pain. "If you say so," he said, leaving his meaning ambiguous.

Annoyed, Piper was anxious to be gone from that too-small room. She wished she hadn't approached the bed, if only because she could see so much of his bare chest. It was disturbing—though it did remind her of the gods and heroes she'd read about in Greek mythology.

She gathered her dignity, an effort of unsettling significance, reached out to reclaim the lantern. "If you don't need anything, I'll leave you to get some rest," she said, speaking as charitably as she could.

"I do need something," he told her quietly.

Piper took another step back. The lantern light wavered slightly, and she renewed her grip on the handle. "What?" she asked cautiously.

"Company," Sawyer replied. "Somebody to talk to while I wait for this bullet hole in my shoulder to settle down a little—it feels like somebody dropped a hot coal into it. Why don't you take a chair—if there is one—and tell me what brings a proper lady like you to a rough town like Blue River."

Was he making fun of her, using the term "a proper lady" ironically?

Or was she being not only harsh, but priggish, too?

She set the lantern back on the night table and drew her rocking chair into the faint circle of light, sat down and folded her hands in her lap. For the moment, that was all the concession she could bring herself to make. And it seemed like plenty.

"Well?" Sawyer McKettrick prompted. "I can tell by the way you talk and carry yourself that you're an Easterner. What are you doing way out here in the wilds of Texas?"

"I told you," Piper said distantly, primly. "I teach school."

"They don't have schools back where you came from, in Massachusetts or New Hampshire or wherever you belong?"

"I'm from Maine, if you must know," she allowed, suppressing an urge to argue that she "belonged" wherever she wanted to be. "Dara Rose—Clay's wife—is my cousin. She persuaded me to come out here and take over for the last teacher, Miss Krenshaw."

"Dara Rose," he said, with a fond little smile. "Clay's a lucky man, finding a woman like her."

"I quite agree," Piper said, softening toward him, albeit unwillingly and only to a minimal degree.

He studied her thoughtfully in the flickering light of the lantern. "Does it suit you—life in the Wild West, I mean?" he inquired politely. She saw that a muscle had bunched in his jaw after he spoke, knew he was hurting, and determined to ride it out without complaint. Like Clay, he was tough, though Clay wore the quality with greater grace, being a more reticent sort.

Piper paused, considering her reply. "It's lonely sometimes," she admitted, at last.

"Everyplace is lonely sometimes," he answered.

This was a statement Piper couldn't refute, so she made one of her own. "It sounds as if you speak from experience," she said carefully.

He grinned a wan shadow of a grin, lifted his right hand in a gesture of acquiescence. "Sure," he replied. "Happens to everybody."

Even in his weakened state, Sawyer McKettrick did not strike Piper as the kind of person who ever lacked for anything. There was something about him, some quality of quiet sufficiency, of untroubled wholeness, that shone even through his obvious physical discomfort.

"I do enjoy spending my days with the children," she said, strangely flustered, sensing that there was far more to this man than what showed on the surface.

"I reckon that's a good thing, since you're a teacher," he observed dryly.

A silence fell, and Piper found herself wanting to prattle, just to fill it. And she was most definitely *not* a prattler, so this was a matter for concern.

"I might be able to handle some food, after all," Sawyer ventured presently, unhurriedly. "If the offer is still good, that is."

Relieved to have an errand to perform, however mundane, Piper fairly leaped to her feet, took the lamp by its handle. "There's bean soup," she said. "I'll get you some."

When she returned with a bowl and spoon in one hand and the lantern in the other, she saw that her visitor had bunched up the pillows behind him so he could sit up straighter.

She placed the lantern on the night table again and extended the bowl and spoon.

He looked at the food with an expression of amused wistfulness. "I've only got one good arm," he reminded her. "I can feed myself, but you'll have to hold the bowl."

Piper should have anticipated this development, but she hadn't. Gingerly, knowing she wouldn't be able to reach far enough from the rocking chair, she sat down on the edge of the mattress, the bowl cupped in both hands.

The sure impropriety of the act sent a little thrill through her.

Deep down, she was something of a rebel, though she managed to hide that truth from most people.

Sawyer smiled and took hold of the spoon, tasted the soup. Since the fire in the stove had burned low while they were talking earlier, the stuff was only lukewarm, but he didn't seem to mind. He ate slowly, and not very much, and finally sank back against the pillows, looking exhausted by the effort of feeding himself.

"Would you like more?" Piper ventured, drawing back the bowl. "I could—"

Sawyer grimaced, shook his head no. His skin was a waxy shade of gray, even in the thin light, and he seemed to be bleeding from his wound again, though not so heavily as before. "That'll do for now," he said. "I might take some laudanum, after all, though."

Piper nodded, put the spoon and the bowl down, and reached for the brown bottle Dr. Howard had left, pulled out the cork. "I'll just wipe off the spoon and—"

Before she could finish her sentence, though, he grabbed the bottle from her hand and took a great draught from it. The muscles in his neck corded visibly as he swallowed.

Piper blinked and snatched the vessel from him. "Mr. *McKettrick,*" she scolded, in her most teacherly voice. "That is *medicine,* not water, and it's very potent."

"I hope so," he said with a sigh, closing his eyes and gritting his teeth. Waiting for the opium to reach his bloodstream. "I'd have preferred whiskey," he added, moments later.

Soon, he was fast asleep.

Piper made sure the bottle of laudanum was out of his reach and rose to carry the lantern and the bowl and spoon out of the room, walking softly so she wouldn't wake him—not that there seemed to be much danger of that, from the steady rasp of his breathing.

Once she'd set the bowl and spoon aside, along with the lantern, she wrapped one of the extra blankets Dr. Howard had brought around her shoulders, in lieu of a cloak, and marched herself outside, into the snowy cold, carrying the lantern again now, lighting her way to the outhouse. Normally, she would have used the enamel chamber pot tucked beneath her bed, but not this time.

The going was hard, though not quite as arduous as when she'd gone out for wood and water before, and to take care of Mr. McKettrick's horse. She heard a reassuring dripping sound—snow melting off the eaves of the schoolhouse roof, probably—and the sky was clear and moonlit and speckled with stars.

For the time being at least, the storm was over, and that heartened Piper so much that, after using the outhouse, she went on to the shed, where the big buckskin gelding stood, quietly munching hay.

She spoke to him companionably, stroked his sturdy neck a few times, and made sure he had enough water. Clay had filled the trough earlier, instead of just setting a pail on the dirt floor of the shed, so there was plenty.

Returning to the schoolhouse, Piper set the lantern down, put the covered kettle of boiled beans on the front step, so the cold would keep its contents from spoiling. Then she shut the door, lowered the latch, and went over to bank the fire for the night.

The lamp was starting to burn low by then, so she quickly made herself a bed on the floor, using the borrowed blankets, washed her face and hands in a basin of warm water, and brushed her teeth with baking soda. Donning one of her flannel nightgowns was out of the question, of course, with a man under the same roof.

Resigned to sleeping in her clothes, she put out the lamp and stretched out on the floor, as near to the stove as she could safely get, and bundled herself in the blankets. The planks were hard, and Piper thought with yearning of her thin, lumpy mattress, the one she'd so often complained about, though only to herself and Dara Rose.

She closed her eyes, depending on

exhaustion to carry her into the unknow-
ing solace of sleep, but instead she found
herself listening, not just with her ears, but
with all she was. A few times, she thought
she heard small feet skittering and scurry-
ing around her, which didn't help her state
of mind.

At some point, however, she finally succumbed to a leaden, dreamless slumber.

When she awakened on that frosty floor,
sore and unrested and quite disgruntled, it
took her a few moments to remember why
she was there, and not in her bed.

The bed was *occupied,* she recalled,
with a flare of heat rising to her cheeks. By
one Sawyer McKettrick.

But the sun was shining, and that lifted
her spirits considerably.

She shambled stiffly to her feet, hurried
to build up the fire in the potbellied stove,
glanced with mild alarm at the big Regulator clock ticking on the schoolhouse wall.
It was past eight, she saw, and she hadn't
rung the schoolhouse bell.

A silly concern, admittedly, since her
students weren't likely to show up, even
though the snow had stopped falling and

cheery daylight filled the frigid little room, absorbing the blue shadows of a wintry yesterday and the night that had followed. At the front window, Piper used the palm of one hand, no longer sore, to wipe a circle in the curlicues of frost to clear the glass. She peered out, encouraged to see that the sky was indeed blue and virtually cloudless.

Moisture dripped steadily from the roof overhead, and the road was taking shape again, a slight but visible dip in the deep, blindingly white field of snow that seemed to stretch on and on.

The voice, coming from behind her, wry and somewhat testy, nearly caused Piper to jump out of her skin. For a few moments, glorying in the change in the weather, she'd forgotten all about her uninvited guest, her night on the floor, and most of her other concerns, as well.

"Is there any coffee in this place, or would that be sinful, like keeping a stock of whiskey?" Sawyer McKettrick asked grumpily.

Piper whirled, saw him standing— *standing,* under his own power—in the doorway to her private quarters. He was still bare-chested, his bandages bulky and his bad arm in the sling Doc had improvised for him the day before, but, thankfully, he'd somehow managed to get into his trousers and even put on his boots.

He looked pale, gaunt, but ready for whatever challenges the day—or the next few minutes—might bring.

She smiled, relieved. If Sawyer was up and around, he'd be leaving soon. Maybe *very* soon. "I'll make some coffee," she said. "Sit down."

He was leaning against the framework of the doorway now, probably conserving his strength, and he looked around, taking in the small desks, the benches. "Where?" he asked, practically snarling the word.

Piper was determined to be pleasant, no matter how rude Mr. McKettrick chose to be. "There's a chair behind my desk," she pointed out. "Take that."

He groped his way along the wall, proof that he wasn't as recovered as she'd first thought, pulled back the wooden chair and sank into it. "Where's my shirt?" he asked. "And my .45?"

Piper ladled water into the small enamel

coffeepot that, like the three drinking mugs, her narrow bed and the rocking chair, came with the schoolhouse. "I burned your shirt," she said cheerfully. "It was quite ruined, between the bullet hole and all the blood. And I put away the pistol, since you won't have use for it here."

Sawyer thrust his free hand through his hair in exasperation. Clearly, the laudanum had worn off, and he hadn't rested well. "I need that shirt," he said. *"And* the .45."

"I'm sorry," Piper answered. "Perhaps Clay will bring you fresh clothes, when he comes to take you out to the ranch." She refused to discuss the gun any further.

Sawyer frowned. His chin was bristly with beard stubble, and he narrowed his blue-green eyes practically to slits. "When will that be?" he growled. "My trunk is over at the train depot. Plenty of clothes in there."

Piper didn't reply right away, since she didn't know precisely when Clay would return, and fetching Sawyer's baggage from the depot was not presently an option. Instead, she put some coffee beans into the grinder and turned the handle, enjoying the rich scent as it rose to entice her. Coffee was normally a treat for Piper, though she'd been drinking more of it lately, being snowed in and everything. Since the stuff wasn't considered a staple, like canned goods and meat, potatoes and butter, the town didn't provide it as a part of her wages. Since she saved practically every penny toward a train ticket home to Maine, Dara Rose bought it for her, along with writing paper, postage stamps and bathing soap.

God bless Dara Rose's generous soul.

Sawyer cleared his throat, a reminder, apparently, that she'd neglected to answer his cranky question. "Clay will be coming back—when?"

"I don't know," Piper said honestly. "Soon, I hope."

His frown deepened as he looked around again. "Where did you sleep last night?"

She measured coffee into the pot and set it on the stove to boil. "You needn't concern yourself with that," she said sunnily.

He gave a gruff chortle at her response,

completely void of amusement. Then he pushed back the chair and stood, with an effort he clearly wanted very much to hide. "I suppose the privy is out back?" he asked.

Piper kept her face averted, so he wouldn't see her blush. "Yes," she said. "But the snow is deep and the path hasn't been cleared yet." She paused, mortified. "There's a chamber pot under the bed."

"I'm not using a chamber pot," he informed her, each word separated from the next by a tick of the Regulator clock. Slowly, he crossed the room, snatched up the same blanket she'd used earlier, in lieu of a coat, wrapped it around his mostly naked upper body like an enormous shawl, and left the schoolhouse.

The door slammed behind him.

Piper hoped he wouldn't collapse in the snow again, because she wasn't sure she'd be able to get him back inside the schoolhouse if that happened. She waited tensely, added water to the coffeepot when it bubbled, and resisted the urge to stand at the window and watch for his return.

He did reappear, after a few minutes,

and he kept the blanket around him as he made his way back to the desk chair and sat down.

Piper poured coffee for him—the grounds hadn't settled completely, but that couldn't be helped—and set the mug on the surface of the desk.

"Breakfast?" she asked.

He finally smiled, though grudgingly. "More beans?" he countered.

"I have some salt pork and a few eggs," Piper responded. "Would that do, or should I risk life and limb to fetch something more to your liking from the hotel dining room? I could just hitch up the dogsled and be off."

He laughed, and it seemed that his color was a little better, though that could probably be ascribed to the cold weather outside. "You don't lack for sass, do you?" he said.

"And *you* don't lack for rudeness," Piper retorted, but, like before, she was softening toward him a little. There was something about that smile, those intelligent, blue-green eyes, that supple mouth . . .

Whoa, ordered a voice in her mind,

bringing her up short. *Forget his smile, and his mouth, too.* Silently, Piper reminded herself that, to her knowledge, Sawyer McKettrick had just one thing to recommend him—that he was Clay's cousin—which most definitely did *not* mean he was the same kind of man. Families, even ones as illustrious as Clay's, *did* have black sheep.

"Sorry," he said wearily, with no hint of actual remorse.

She fetched the salt pork and the eggs, which were kept in a metal storage box in the cloakroom, that being the coldest part of the building, and proceeded to prepare breakfast for both of them.

"There's a little house for the marshal to live in," she said busily, after a few stiff minutes had passed. "The town provides it."

"I know," Sawyer said. "I was here in Blue River once before." Now that he had coffee to drink, his temperament seemed to be improving. A hot meal might render him tolerable. "Dara Rose lived there at the time, with her daughters."

"Oh," Piper said, apropos of nothing, turning slices of salt pork in the skillet, then cracking three eggs into the same pan, causing them to sizzle in the melted lard.

"These accommodations of yours are pretty rustic," he said, evidently to make conversation, which Piper could have done without just then. "The bed feels like a rock pile, and there's no place to take a bath."

Piper, who yearned for an indoor bathroom like the one Dara Rose had now, in her lovely new ranch house, and a feather bed, and many other things in the bargain, took umbrage. *These accommodations of hers,* humble as they were, had very probably saved his life. "I manage just fine," she said coolly.

Sawyer sighed wearily. "I didn't mean it as an insult," he said.

Piper plopped the salt pork and two of the eggs onto a tin plate—also provided by the good people of Blue River—and carried it over to him, along with a knife and fork.

She set the works down with an eloquent clatter and rested her hands on her hips.

"Would you like more coffee?" she demanded inhospitably.

He grinned up at her, enjoying her pique. "Yes, ma'am, I would," he said. "If you please."

She stormed back to the stove, took up a pot holder, and brought the coffee to the desk that doubled as a table. There was a heavy clunking sound as the base of it met the splintery oak surface.

"Thank you," the new marshal said sweetly.

"You're welcome," she crabbed.

A knock sounded at the schoolhouse door just then, and hope filled Piper, displacing her irritation and her strangely injured pride. Perhaps Clay had returned, or Doc Howard—

But when she answered the firm rap, she found Bess Turner standing on the step, looking poised to flee if the need arose. Bess ran the brothel above the Bitter Gulch Saloon, and if she'd ever tried to look respectable, she'd given up on it long ago.

Her hair was a brassy shade of yellow, her thin cheeks were heavily rouged, and her mouth was hard, not with anger, Piper had often thought, but with the strain of bearing up under one tribulation and sorrow after another.

"I'm sorry to bother you," Bess said, almost meekly. She wore a pink satin cloak, completely inadequate for a December day, and her dancing shoes were soaked through.

"Come in," Piper said quickly, stepping back. "There's coffee made—I'll pour you some."

Bess's tired gaze strayed past Piper, dusted over Sawyer, and came back to Piper again. "Thank you," she said, very quietly.

"Stand over here by the stove," Piper urged, with a shiver, hastening to rinse out a coffee cup. "You must be freezing!"

Bess sidled close to the fire, and Piper noticed that the woman's hands were gloveless, and blue with cold. "I can't stay long," she said, stealing another glance at Sawyer. Naturally, she'd be curious about his presence, but she wasn't likely to carry tales, like some of the other townswomen would have done. "My Ginny-Sue is hectoring me something fierce about the Christmas program," she added fretfully. "She's learned the whole second chapter of Luke by heart, that being her piece for the recital, and she's afraid school won't take up again before then, because of the snow."

Piper was touched. Ginny-Sue, a shy ten-year-old, was one of her brightest pupils. Except for Madeline Howard, she was the best-dressed, too, always neatly clad in ready-made dresses, with her face scrubbed and her brown hair plaited. Her shoes were the envy of the other girls, sturdy, but with buttons instead of laces, and always polished to a high shine.

"Christmas is still more than a week away," Piper said gently, handing Bess the coffee. "I'm sure we won't have to cancel the program."

Bess nodded, looking straight at Sawyer now and making no effort to hide her curiosity. "Now, who would you be?" she asked him, straight out.

He'd risen to his feet, abandoning his breakfast for the moment. "Name's Sawyer McKettrick," he answered cordially. "I'm the new town marshal."

"He's Clay's cousin," Piper added hastily, as though that explained what he was doing in the schoolhouse at this hour of the

morning, wearing nothing but boots, trousers and a blanket.

"Howdy," said the local madam. "I'm
Bess Turner. Miss St. James here teaches
my girl, Ginny-Sue."

Sawyer dropped back into his chair.
"Good to meet you," he said, and resumed
eating, though he continued to take an un-
disguised interest in the visitor.

"He was shot," Piper went on anxiously.
"Clay and Dr. Howard said he couldn't be
moved, so he spent the night here—"

Bess smiled, and a twinkle appeared in
her faded eyes, just for the briefest moment. "Shot, was he?" she replied, looking
Sawyer over again, this time more thoroughly. "You'd never guess it."

Piper thought of Dara Rose's late husband, who had died in Bess's establish-
ment, and wondered if the two of them
had been together at the time of his scandalous demise. Not that she'd ever be so
forward as to ask, of course. There were
some things a body had to be content to
wonder about in perpetuity.

Piper looked back at Sawyer, who moved
the blanket aside just enough to show the

bandage and part of his sling. He'd guessed that she was embarrassed, evidently, and the fact seemed to amuse him.

"Did you see who shot you?" Bess asked. It was a question Piper hadn't thought to ask, and neither, as far as she knew, had Clay or Doc Howard.

"The snow was too thick," Sawyer answered, with a shake of his head.

"Well, I'll be," marveled Bess, finishing her coffee. "Blue River's always been a peaceful town, for the most part. I hope we're not drawing in all sorts of riffraff, like some other places I could name."

The corner of Sawyer's well-made mouth quirked up in a semblance of a grin, probably at the term "riffraff," coming from someone like Bess, but he didn't say anything.

Bess handed over the empty mug and smiled at Piper. "So I can tell my Ginny-Sue there'll still be a Christmas?" she asked.

"I'm sure of it," Piper said, though that was mostly bravado. Inwardly, she wasn't so sure that the warmer weather would hold—but she *hoped* it would, and fiercely.

Bess nodded a farewell to Sawyer and walked purposely toward the door, Piper following.

On the threshold, Bess paused, lowered her voice and said, "If you need any help, Teacher, just send word over to the Bitter Gulch. My girls and me, we'll do whatever we can to lend a hand."

Piper's throat tightened, and the backs of her eyes burned a little. She wondered how many of the other women of Blue River, besides Dara Rose, of course, would have made such an offer. "Thank you, Mrs. Turner," she said warmly.

"Bess," the other woman corrected, patting Piper's hand before taking her leave. "I never was nobody's missus, and I won't pretend I was."

With that, she started down the slippery steps of the schoolhouse porch, drawing her tawdry cloak more closely around her. The sun glinted in her dandelion-colored hair, and she looked back at Piper, smiled once more, and waved.

Piper waved back, and closed the door slowly.

When she turned around, she saw that Sawyer had finished his breakfast. Still seated at her desk, he watched her over the rim of his coffee mug.

"Christmas," he said, in a musing tone, his gaze skimming over the undecorated tree leaning forlornly against the far wall, slowly but surely dropping its needles. Piper had sent the bigger boys out to find it the previous week, thinking they'd all be able to enjoy it longer that way, though now she wished she'd waited. "I forgot all about it."

"You'll be at Clay and Dara Rose's place by then," Piper said, holding on to blind faith that it would be so, "probably much mended."

"I'll need to round up some presents for those little girls," Sawyer mused.

"I wouldn't worry," Piper counseled, liking him again. Sort of. "They're well provided for, Edrina and Harriet."

He smiled. "Yes," he said. "They would be, with Clay for a father."

The remark stung Piper a little, on Dara Rose's behalf, dampening her kindly inclination toward Mr. McKettrick, even though she sensed no rancor in the remark. Her cousin had had a difficult life, almost from the first, but Dara Rose was and always had been a devoted mother. "If Clay were here," she said moderately, "he'd tell you that he's the fortunate one."

Sawyer sighed. He looked paler than before, though breakfast and the coffee must have braced him up. "I've managed to get on the wrong side of you again," he said. "I *know* Clay loves his wife, and he considers those girls his own, as much as he does the baby he and Dara Rose are expecting."

Piper bit her lower lip for a moment. "I apologize," she said. "I didn't sleep very well last night, and I confess that I'm worried that I might have spoken out of turn to Bess Turner—" She paused, swallowed. "If there's another storm, Christmas will have to be canceled and the children will be so disappointed."

His grin flashed again, brief but bright as the sunlight on the snow outside. "Christmas happens in the heart," he said. "*Especially* the heart of a child."

She regarded him for a long moment. "That's a lovely sentiment," she said, taken by surprise, "and I'm sure it's true, for fortunate children like Edrina and Harriet, and

Doc Howard's little girl, Madeline, but there are others, like Ginny-Sue Turner, who need more." She inclined her head toward the forlorn little tree, leaning against the schoolhouse wall. "They need the sparkle and the carols, the excitement and, yes, the oranges and the peppermint sticks, because the other three-hundred-sixty-four days of the year can be bleak for them."

Sawyer, clearly tiring, leaned against the framework of the bedroom doorway again, and smiled sadly. "You really care about these kids," he said.

"Of course I do," Piper replied.

"What do *you* want for Christmas, Miss St. James?" he asked quietly.

She hadn't thought of her own secret wishes for a long time, and the question unsettled her. "You need to rest," she hedged. "Go in and lie down."

"Not until I get an answer," he replied, folding his good arm across the sling that held his injured one in place.

Piper blushed. "Very well, then," she said, throwing out the first thing that came to mind so he would drop the subject and leave her in peace. "I'd like a new cloak, since you bled all over mine and I had to burn all but a few scraps of it."

Sawyer McKettrick smiled again. "Done," he said. And then he turned around and went back to bed.

CHAPTER 4

Clay returned shortly after noon, at the reins of a sledge improvised from lengths of lumber, probably left over from the building of his house and barn, with two enormous plow horses hitched to the front. He grinned and waved when Piper stepped out onto the schoolhouse porch, shielding her eyes from the bright sun with one hand.

"How's that ornery cousin of mine faring?" he called, bringing the team to a halt. The back of the sledge was piled high with an assortment of things—crates and boxes, a supply of hay for Sawyer's horse, a few bulging feed bags and, most notably, the parts of an iron bedstead and a mattress secured with rope.

"He was up and around earlier," Piper replied, staring at the bedstead and wondering whether Clay planned to leave it at the schoolhouse for her or use it to transport Sawyer to the ranch, "but he's resting at the moment."

"Up and around?" Clay echoed, pleased. He climbed off the strange conveyance and approached through the knee-deep but already-melting snow. "I guess I shouldn't be surprised. Sawyer always had more gumption than good sense."

"He's wanting his trunk from the depot," Piper said, as Clay reached her and she stepped back so they could both go inside, where it was warmer.

"I figured as much," Clay told her, taking off his hat and hanging it from a peg near the door. He'd stomped most of the snow off his boots out on the porch. "Picked it up before I came here."

Sawyer, who must have heard the commotion, appeared in the doorway to Piper's room, looking rumpled and grim. He obviously needed more laudanum, and

Piper made up her mind to fetch it and supervise the dosage this time, make sure he didn't guzzle the stuff down again.

"You ready to make the trip out to our place?" Clay asked his cousin, looking doubtful even as he spoke. "I can haul you out there today if you want to go, and in style, too, like Caesar reclining on Cleopatra's barge."

Piper felt a pang of sadness at the thought of Sawyer's leaving the schoolhouse, which was just plain silly, because she ought to be relieved instead. She *really* ought to be relieved.

Sawyer frowned, puzzlement personified. "Caesar? Cleopatra's barge? What the devil are you yammering on about?"

"Either way, I came prepared," was all the answer Clay gave. He was still grinning, proud of his resourcefulness, and he waxed unusually loquacious, for him. "I brought along a kind of sleigh I rigged up last year, out of some old boards—normally use it to haul feed out to the cattle on the range when the wagons can't get through—even brought a bed along, in case you were ready to head out to the ranch sooner than expected. There's hay and some grain for your gelding, too, if you'd rather stay put a while longer. In that case, I'll set the bedstead up for Piper, so she won't have to sleep on the floor until you're out of her hair."

Piper blinked.

"You slept on the floor?" Sawyer asked, practically glowering at her, as though accusing her of some unconscionable perfidy.

"Where did you *think* she was sleeping?" Clay inquired good-naturedly. "This is a one-room schoolhouse, Sawyer, not a big-city hospital or a grand hotel."

"I cannot have a bed in my schoolroom," Piper put in hastily, though neither man seemed to be listening.

"I'll go back with you," Sawyer said to Clay, though when he took a step, he winced and swayed on his feet so that his cousin immediately stepped forward and took him by the arms, lest he collapse.

Sawyer flinched and his face drained of color.

Chagrined, Clay loosened his grip, though he didn't dare let go completely. "I don't believe you're ready quite yet," he said reasonably.

"My .45," Sawyer said, looking dazed. "She—took it."

"Never mind that," Clay told him. "Right now, we've got to get you back to bed."

Sawyer allowed himself to be turned around and led in the other direction, most likely because he didn't have much choice in the matter. "My *pistol,*" he insisted.

Piper glanced toward the cloakroom, where she'd hidden the weapon, climbing onto the food box to push it to the back of a wide, high shelf. She wanted that dreadful thing out of sight *and* out of reach, so none of her students would stumble upon it, once they returned to school, and bring about a tragedy.

For all that, something in Sawyer's tone bothered her. Was he afraid the man who had shot him would return, make another attempt on his life and, this time, succeed in killing him?

Maybe, she concluded, but the fact remained that Sawyer wasn't in his right mind, given all the blood he'd lost and the pain he'd suffered. By now, the shooter was surely putting as many miles as he could between himself and Blue River, no doubt believing that his quarry was dead.

She shuddered, hugged herself against an inner chill.

What if she was wrong? What if, by hiding the gun, she was putting both Sawyer and herself in danger?

In the next room, Clay murmured something, and then the bedsprings creaked as Sawyer lay down again.

Piper paced. She'd ask Clay what to do with the gun when he came back.

He took his time, though, speaking quietly to Sawyer, probably giving him laudanum from Doc's bottle. By the time he returned to the schoolroom, Piper had reheated the coffee left over from breakfast and poured some into a mug for him.

"Thanks," Clay said, accepting the cup and taking a restorative sip before going on. "Has Doc been back? Sawyer's in bad shape."

Piper shook her head no. "He'll be here," she said, with confidence. Weather or no weather, Doc Howard was not the kind to stay away when he was needed. "Clay—?"

He raised one eyebrow. "If you're worried about me setting up that bedstead in the schoolroom—"

Again, she shook her head. "Sawyer's been asking for his gun," she said. "I put it away, but now I'm wondering if I ought to give it back to him. In case—in case—"

Clay's expression was a solemn one. "Where is it?" he asked.

She led the way into the cloakroom and pointed upward.

Clay was so tall that he didn't need anything to stand on to reach the Colt .45 in its hiding place. He extended one hand, felt around a little, and found the pistol. Bringing it down to eye level, he examined it, expertly checking the cylinder to see that there were bullets inside.

"Better give it back to him," he said. "I know Sawyer, and he won't get any real rest as long as this thing is out of his reach."

Piper's heart pounded. "But—" She paused, swallowed, tried again. "He's not himself. What if he doesn't recognize you or me or Doc and shoots someone?"

To Piper's surprise, Clay chuckled, though it was a raspy sound, not really an expression of amusement. "Sawyer's himself, all right," he assured her. "Always is, no matter what. And he won't shoot anybody who isn't fixing to shoot *him,* no matter how delirious he might be."

"How can you be so sure?" Piper persisted. She hated guns. These were modern times, for heaven's sake, and they were not the Old West but the new one.

"I know my cousin," Clay replied matter-of-factly. "We grew up together, he and I. He's been shooting almost as long as he's been riding horses, and he showed a unique talent for it from the first."

Again, Piper shuddered. "You're saying that he's a—a gunslinger?"

"I'm saying he's good with a gun. There's a difference."

"But what if he's a criminal? You've said it yourself—no one is sure, including you, that Sawyer isn't an outlaw."

Clay held the pistol carefully but competently, keeping the barrel pointed toward the floor as he passed her, leaving the cloakroom. "Even if he *is* an outlaw," he replied easily, "he wouldn't shoot anybody down in cold blood. He's also a *McKettrick,* after all."

Piper was exasperated. The McKettrick family had their own distinct code of ethics, hammered out by the patriarch, Angus, and handed down to his sons and their sons after them, but it seemed obvious that Sawyer might not subscribe to that honorable philosophy, given his secrecy about his vocation. On the other hand, Clay trusted his cousin enough to hand over his own badge, and that was no small matter.

Clay carried the pistol to Sawyer's bedside and came back, intent on the next task. "I'll see to my cousin's horse," he said, "and unload the supplies."

Doc Howard showed up while Clay was outside, and the two of them carried the bedstead and mattress, still roped together, into the schoolhouse.

The bed wasn't very wide—it probably belonged to either Edrina or Harriet—but there was no room for it in front, so they took it into the teacher's quarters. Piper fussed and hovered like a hen chased away from its nest, but Clay only said, "You can't sleep on the floor," and proceeded to set the thing up in the little space available—crosswise at the foot of the bed where Sawyer lay, sound asleep.

It made a T-shape, and Piper figured that T stood for *trouble*.

"You'll be quite safe," Doc added, in fatherly tones, after helping Clay assemble the second bed. Sawyer's eyelids fluttered, but he didn't stir otherwise. The pistol rested, a daunting presence in its own right, on the night table. "Mr. McKettrick here is an invalid, remember."

An invalid? Piper thought. Sawyer had gotten out of bed without help just that morning, visited the shed where his horse was kept as well as the privy, and returned to the schoolhouse with enough strength to drink coffee and eat breakfast.

"Safe?" Piper challenged, folding her arms. "By now, my reputation must be in tatters."

"Nobody knows Sawyer's here," Clay reasoned, unwinding the rope that left a deep dent in the middle of the bed. "I haven't said a word to anybody but Dara Rose. She sent some things for you, by the way, staples, mostly, and a book she ordered from back East. Says she'll read it when you're finished."

Piper thought of her cousin with both gratitude and frustration. If only Dara Rose were here, too. As a respectable married woman, she could have defused any gossip by her mere presence.

Doc wouldn't look at Piper, though it took her a moment to notice, and when she did, she saw that his neck had reddened above his tight celluloid collar. He'd told Eloise, of course—his wife would have demanded an explanation for his leaving the house when everyone else was staying home, close to the fire.

"Doc?" Piper prodded suspiciously.

"I've sworn Mrs. Howard to secrecy," he said, but he still wouldn't meet her gaze.

Some things, like a mysterious man occupying the schoolmarm's bed, ablebodied or not, were simply too deliciously improper to keep silent about, especially for people like Eloise Howard. Bess Turner, by ironic contrast, wouldn't say a word to anyone—Piper was sure of that.

She groaned aloud.

"It's too late anyhow," Clay observed lightly, straightening after he'd crouched to tighten a screw in the framework of the bedstead. "If there's damage to your good name, it's already been done."

Piper flung out her hands. "Well," she

sputtered, "thank you very much for *that,*
Clay McKettrick. But why should *you*
worry? *You're* not the one who'll wind up
an old maid and maybe even lose her job!"

He chuckled and shoved a hand through
his dark hair. "I reckon it's a certainty that
I'll never be an old maid," he conceded.
"But you probably won't, either. There aren't
so many women way out here that men
can afford to be choosy."

Doc Howard closed his eyes, shook his
head.

Piper would have shrieked at Clay if it
hadn't been for Sawyer, placidly sleeping
nearby. She didn't want to startle him
awake—he might grab for his pistol then
and shoot them all.

"Choosy?" she fired back, in a ferocious
whisper.

Doc Howard put a hand to each of their
backs and steered both Clay and Piper
out into the schoolroom. "Now, Clay," the
dentist said, in a diplomatic tone meant to
pour oil on troubled waters, "any man
would be proud to have a lovely woman
like Piper here for a wife. Piper, Clay's
going to pull his foot out of his mouth any

moment now and apologize for the thought-less remark he just made."

Clay did look sorry. Deflated, too. "I didn't mean that the way it sounded," he said. "I do ask your pardon." When Piper just glared at him, not saying a word in reply, he sighed miserably, turned and headed outside, ostensibly to bring in Sawyer's trunk and the things Dara Rose had sent in from the ranch.

Doc smiled and touched her upper arm. "There, now," he told her. "Matters are rarely as bad as they seem."

Piper opened her mouth, closed it again, remembering childhood counsel. If she didn't have something nice to say, she shouldn't say anything at all.

"I'm going back in there to check the wound and change the bandages," Doc said, leaving Sawyer himself completely out of the equation, it seemed to Piper.

She busied herself building up the fire. Clay carried in a crate filled with supplies, and she spotted not only the promised book, one she'd been yearning to read, but a bag of coffee beans, tea leaves in a tin canister, several jars of preserves, two loaves of bread, and even part of a ham, with the bone intact, so she could make soup later.

Piper said nothing.

Clay, resigned, went out again, lugged a sizable travel trunk over the threshold and on into the little room that now contained two beds instead of one.

As if she'd consider sleeping in such close proximity to a man, an armed *stranger,* no less, of dubious moral convictions.

Spending another night on the floor wasn't a happy prospect either, though, so she put that out of her mind, along with thoughts of Sawyer McKettrick.

Doc and Clay conferred again, and soon came out of the bedroom, single file. Doc's hands were wet from a recent washing— he must have used the basin on Piper's bureau—and he was rolling down his sleeves, shrugging back into his coat to make his departure.

Most likely, he would go straight home and tell Eloise that the problem of sleeping arrangements over at the schoolhouse had been solved. Now the teacher would have a bed of her very own.

Inwardly, Piper sighed. Doc, having only the best of intentions himself, mistakenly believed that everyone else was the same way.

"I'll tie Cherokee behind the sleigh and lead him out to the ranch," Clay told Piper. "That way, you won't have to worry about feeding and watering him if it snows again."

"Thank you," Piper said crisply. This, it seemed, was Clay's version of appeasement, at least in part. "When will you be back?" The question was addressed to both Clay and Doc Howard.

"I'll get here tomorrow if it's at all possible," Doc promised.

"Soon as I can," Clay said, in his turn. "Dara Rose tells me the baby's dropped a little, says it means we'll have another daughter or a son anytime now, so a lot depends on how she's feeling."

"Maybe Dara Rose would be safer in town," Piper said, fretful again as she thought of her cousin way out there on that lonely ranch, heavily pregnant. "Closer to Doc."

"I'm a *dentist,*" Doc reminded them both.

"You've delivered babies before," Piper

said. It was true; she herself knew of two different occasions when he had served as midwife.

"Only because I didn't have a choice," Doc answered.

"I've brought a few colts and calves into the world," Clay put in, affably confident. "It can't be all that different."

Piper had had enough male wisdom for one day. As much as she dreaded their leaving, a part of her couldn't wait for both Clay *and* Doc to make themselves scarce. Naturally, that meant she'd be alone with Sawyer again, but he slept most of the time anyway.

"Tell Dara Rose I'm grateful for the things she sent to town for me," she said moderately. "Especially the book."

Clay smiled. "She wrote you a letter, too. It's in the box somewhere."

The news heartened Piper, and at the same time made her regret that she hadn't anticipated this and prepared a letter of her own, to send back with Clay. "I hope to see all of you at the Christmas program, if not before then," she said.

Clay looked dubious. "I'll do my best to

bring the girls in for the party, if the weather allows, but I can't see Dara Rose making the trip."

"No," Piper agreed sadly. "I suppose not. She's well, though?"

Clay smiled. "She's just fine, Piper. Don't you worry." His eyes lit up. "Tell you what. If Sawyer's better by then, I'll bring both of you out to the ranch Christmas Eve, after the program, and we'll all celebrate the big day together. I'll even see that you get back to Blue River before school takes up again after New Year's."

"I'd like that," Piper said, cheered. The prospect of spending time with her cousin and the children, holding the baby if it had arrived by then, and, yes, taking long, luxurious baths in Dara Rose's claw-footed tub, complete with hot and cold running water, renewed her.

A few minutes later, after bringing in more water and firewood, Clay and the doctor left.

Piper watched them go through the schoolhouse window, Sawyer's buckskin gelding plodding along behind the team and sled. The sky had gone from blue to gray, she saw with trepidation, but she kept her thoughts in the present moment, since worrying wouldn't do any good.

Emptying the crate Dara Rose had filled for her took up a happy half hour—there were notes from Edrina and Harriet, as well as a long, chatty letter from their mother—and Piper, feeling rich, made herself a pot of tea, lit the lantern against the gathering gloom of a winter afternoon, and sat down at her desk to read.

Dara Rose gave a comical account of ranch life, especially in her current condition, assured Piper that she had nothing to fear from Sawyer McKettrick, and related funny things the children had said. Between the approach of Christmas and being virtually snowed in, Edrina and Harriet had an excess of energy and bickered constantly, settling down only when Clay reminded them that St. Nicholas paid attention to good behavior and dispensed gifts accordingly.

By the time she'd finished reading the letter through for the first time, Piper was both smiling and crying a little. She'd miss Dara Rose and the children terribly if she went back to Maine, she reminded herself silently. They were all the family she had, after all, here *or* there.

Still, in Maine she wouldn't be the school-marm who'd housed a half-naked outlaw, as she would be here in Blue River. She could get another teaching position and eventually meet a suitable man and get married. Finally have a home and children of her own.

A hoarse shout from the bedroom startled her so much that she nearly upset her cup of tea. Alarmed, she bolted to her feet and hurried in to investigate.

Sawyer sat up in bed, breathing hard, his eyes wild, his flesh glistening with perspiration even though the room was fairly cold, being far from the stove. He was holding the pistol in his right hand, and the hammer was drawn back.

For one hysterical moment, Piper thought the shooter must have returned, maybe crawled in through the high window, but there was no one else in the room.

She kept her gaze on the Colt .45 in Sawyer's hand. The barrel was long, and it glinted evilly in the thin light.

"Don't shoot," she said weakly.

Sawyer came back to himself with a visible jolt, blinked a couple of times, and, much to Piper's relief, set the gun aside on the night table. "Sorry," he said. "Guess I must have been dreaming."

Piper lingered in the doorway, waiting for her flailing heart to slow down to its normal pace. Doc had done a good job of replacing Sawyer's bandages; they looked clean and white against his skin. "Are you hungry?" she asked. "Dara Rose sent a lovely ham, and some preserves, too."

He blinked again, then gave a raw chuckle. "You keep asking if I'm hungry," he said. "Why is that?"

"You haven't eaten since breakfast," Piper said, a little defensively. "It's almost suppertime now."

Sawyer looked surprised, and she could tell he was wondering where the day had gone. "It is?" he asked.

"Yes," she said.

"Did Clay bring me any clothes?"

She nodded. "Your trunk is right over there," she said, pointing it out. "Shall I get you something from it?"

He considered the offer. "I'll do it myself," he said. "The way I figure it, the more

I move around, the better off I'll be. Besides, I need to go outside again."

"Your horse is at the ranch," Piper told him. "Clay took it with him when he left."

He grinned. "I know that," he said. "This trip isn't about the horse."

She blushed.

Sawyer swung his legs over the side of the bed. Though the quilt covered his private parts, she couldn't help noticing that he wasn't wearing trousers.

She backed quickly out of the bedroom, followed by the sound of his laughter.

She didn't speak to him or even glance in his direction, minutes later, when he came out of the bedroom, but she knew he was dressed this time, instead of wrapping his upper body in a blanket.

She busied herself heating water—she was desperate for a bath, and planned on locking herself in the cloakroom with her small copper tub later on, when she was sure Sawyer had gone back to sleep—and then sliced Dara Rose's fresh-baked bread and some of the ham, placing the food on plates. She opened a jar of peaches and added those, as well.

Sawyer returned and, forgetting, she

looked his way. Saw that he'd strapped on a gun belt when he got dressed. The handle of the Colt .45 jutted beneath his coat, which was shorter than the ruined one, and just as well made.

"Supper," she said, gesturing toward his full plate, which she'd already carried over to the desk, along with a knife, fork and spoon.

Sawyer nodded in acknowledgment of the one-word invitation, closing the door behind him. "I see there's another bed in the back room," he said. "I was going to offer to sleep on the floor so you wouldn't have to, but I guess that won't be necessary."

Piper was at once touched and flustered by this statement, and turned her head so he wouldn't see that in her face. She wasn't about to discuss the second bed, because she didn't expect to sleep in it, but she kept that to herself, too.

"Clay insisted it would be safe to let you have your pistol back," she said, recalling the look in his eyes when he'd awakened from whatever nightmare he'd been lost in and immediately grabbed the gun, prepared to fire. "I don't mind telling you

that I'm not convinced it was a wise decision."

Sawyer smiled wanly at this, made his
way to her desk, and stood there, looking
bewildered. He was wondering where she
planned to sit, and she hastened, plate
and silverware in hand, to one of the students' places and sat on the bench.

Looking relieved, and singularly worn
out from getting dressed and making the
long slog to and from the outhouse, he
said he'd like to wash up before he ate.

With a nod of her head, she indicated
the basin she'd already filled with warm
water and set on top of a bookshelf, along
with a bar of soap and a towel. While Sawyer cleansed his hands and splashed his
face, she began to eat. The ham and bread
tasted especially good, after a couple of
days of boiled pinto beans, and just the
sight of those lovely peaches, picked in
the autumn from Clay and Dara Rose's
own orchard and put up in their kitchen,
made her mouth water in anticipation.

Sawyer dried his face and hands with
the towel. "I could use a shave," he said,
as he returned to the desk and sat down
to have his supper.

"Maybe tomorrow," Piper replied. The stubble on his chin made him look like the rascal he probably was, but she didn't find it unattractive. She probably should have, though, she thought. Particularly since they were shut in together, the pair of them, and almost certainly raising more of a scandal with every passing day.

And night.

"I'll buy you a new cloak," Sawyer said, out of the blue.

Piper stopped eating, delicious though the food was. "I couldn't accept," she said hurriedly. "It would be improper."

He grinned. "We're way past what's proper already, wouldn't you say?"

It was all too true. Piper colored up again. "You needn't remind me," she said.

The grin held. "I ruined your other cloak, didn't I?" Sawyer asked. "The least I can do is replace it, so you don't freeze to death this winter."

"I'll manage," Piper insisted.

He concentrated on consuming his supper after that, even had a second helping of ham, but his gaze found her every few moments, and each time he looked at her, she saw a twinkle in his eyes.

At last he tired, gathered up his plate and silverware, and looked around for a place to put them.

"I'll take those," Piper said, and did. Since there wasn't a sink in the schoolhouse, she'd wash them later in a basin she reserved for the purpose. By then, she was thinking about the bath she'd take in the cloakroom, once Sawyer had retired to his bed.

Presently, he said good-night and left her alone.

Piper immediately put water on the stove to heat, then hurried outside, to the shed, where she kept the washtub she meant to use.

The snow seemed to be melting, but by the time she returned to the schoolhouse, the hem of her dress was soaked and she was shivering with cold.

It would only be slightly warmer in the cloakroom, she knew, than it was outside, but there was nothing for it. She'd worn these same clothes all of yesterday, then slept in them, and then worn them all day *today*. Now, she felt grimy.

She set the washtub in the cloakroom, filled it bucket by bucket, a process that took a very long time. Sneaking into her bedroom, relieved to see that Sawyer was sleeping peacefully, she collected a flannel nightgown, a washcloth, soap and a towel.

Inside the cloakroom, with a kerosene lantern to light her way, Piper moved the food box in front of the door, just in case, and quickly stripped off her clothes.

Goose bumps sprang up on her bare flesh, and her teeth chattered, but she was resolute. She *would* bathe, even if it was agony, because being dirty was far worse.

The lantern flickered—there was a breeze coming up through the cracks between the planks in the floor—and the bathwater, having taken so long to prepare, was lukewarm when she stepped into it.

Piper scrubbed diligently, dried off with the towel, and donned the flannel nightgown.

The prospect of sleeping on the floor again loomed before her and, as she moved the food box aside, took up the lantern and fled the cloakroom with her discarded day garments wadded up under one elbow, she wondered just how much one small, well-meaning and wholly decent person was meant to endure for the sake of propriety. Especially when that particular horse was already out of the barn, so to speak.

She stopped suddenly when she realized Sawyer was seated at her desk again, wearing half a shirt, since he hadn't been able to put his injured arm through the appropriate sleeve.

He looked up from the book he was reading and smiled. "I wondered if you were shut up in there," he said, with a nod toward the gaping door of the cloakroom. "Even considered coming to your rescue."

"I thought you were asleep," Piper said, still shivering even though—or perhaps *because*—she was wearing her warmest nightgown.

Sawyer's blue-green gaze moved over her like a caress, came back to her face. "Yes," he agreed. "I suppose you did think that. As it happens, though, I woke up and that was that. So I came out here, expecting to find you asleep on the floor, since you're probably too stubborn to use that bed even after all the trouble Clay went to to bring it here."

Piper shifted yesterday's clothes, petticoat, bloomers and camisole included, from her side to her front, like a rumpled shield. "Don't look at me," she said.

He chuckled, averted his eyes. "That's a tall order," he replied, "but whatever else I am, I'm a gentleman, so I'll comply with your request."

"Good," Piper said, not moving.

Sawyer seemed to be reading again, but Piper didn't trust appearances. Nor was she convinced that he was a gentleman.

"Go ahead and take the bedroom," he said. "I'll sleep out here."

CHAPTER 5

"Don't be silly," Piper immediately countered, still clutching her clothes against her bosom. Her nightgown was warm enough, but her bare feet felt icy against the planks, where she seemed to be rooted. "You're in no condition to sleep on a hard floor."

Sawyer, remaining at her desk with a book open in front of him, smiled and carefully kept his gaze averted. Or so she hoped—desperately.

"Neither are you, I'll wager," he said dryly. "Anyhow, I saw a mouse run through here a few minutes ago. Bold little critter, too—scampered right through the middle of the room."

Piper shuddered, and not just from the cold. She had a horror of things that crawled, slithered or scurried, though she'd kept that information to herself in case any of the rambunctious boys in her class got ideas about scaring Teacher with a garter snake or any other objectionable creature.

"What kind of name is Piper, anyhow?" Sawyer asked, turning the pages of the book so rapidly that he couldn't possibly be reading from them.

"What kind of name is Sawyer?" she countered, edging toward the stove. If she'd stayed put, she was convinced the soles of her feet would attach themselves to the icy floor. And where, at this precise moment, was that mouse he'd mentioned seeing?

He chuckled. "I'm named after a great-uncle on my mother's side of the family," he confessed. His lashes were long, she noticed, the same shade of toasty gold as his hair. "My folks—Kade and Mandy McKettrick—had three girls before me, so

I reckon they were prepared to call me Mary Ellen."

In spite of herself, Piper laughed. She was warmer now, standing so near the stove, but no less embarrassed to be wearing nothing but a nightgown. Oddly, the sensation was not completely unpleasant. "You have three sisters?"

Sawyer nodded. "How about you? Do you have sisters or brothers?"

"I'm an only child," Piper said. *And an orphan,* added a voice in her mind. "Dara Rose and I were raised together, though, so we're as close as sisters."

"That's good," Sawyer responded. He cleared his throat. "Aren't you cold?" he asked.

Piper *was* cold, though the proximity of the stove helped a little. Suddenly, no matter what the shameful implications, she realized she couldn't bear the idea of sleeping on the floor again. "Do you promise to conduct yourself like a gentleman if I agree to spend the night in the spare bed?" she asked, horrified to hear herself uttering such a thing.

Sawyer lifted his good arm, palm out,

as if swearing an oath in a court of law. "You have my word," he said.

Piper started for the bedroom doorway, giving him as wide a berth as she could in such a small, cramped space. "Wait until I say it's all right before you come in," she said.

Suppressing a grin, he nodded his agreement.

And Piper dashed past him, into the room that had been hers and hers alone, until night before last. Using sheets and blankets provided by Dara Rose, along with the bed itself and the lovely supper she and Sawyer had shared that evening, Piper quickly made up a cozy nest. Then, driven by the continuing cold and the shock of her own brazen boldness, she scrambled under the covers and lay there shivering until she'd adjusted to the chill of the sheets.

"I'm—ready," she sang out, after a long time.

She saw the light from the lanterns, the one she'd used in the cloakroom and the one Sawyer had been reading by, blink out. He appeared in the doorway, a shadow etched against the darkness, and Piper's heart began to pound so that she dared not speak, lest her voice tremble and betray the nervous excitement she felt.

Sawyer moved through the room, with only a slant of moonlight to see by, and, with an effort Piper could hear from beneath her blankets, took off his clothes. She heard the springs creak as he sat down on the other bed.

"Good night, Miss St. James," he said, with a smile in his voice. "And sleep well."

Piper didn't answer. She was hoping he'd think she was already asleep.

Closing her eyes, she pretended as hard as she could.

LYING THERE IN the darkness, Sawyer cupped his right hand behind his head and smiled up at the ceiling, recalling the delicious look of surprise on Piper St. James's very pretty face a little while before, when she came bursting out of the cloakroom in her nightdress and found him reading at her desk. Her mouth had been blue with cold at the time, and he'd wanted to wrap her up in a blanket—or better yet, his arms—to warm her.

Given her schoolmarm-skittishness, he

reckoned that would have been about the worst thing he could do, but knowing that didn't stop him from imagining the way she'd fit against him, curvy and soft against his own hard lines and angles.

The sensual image tightened his groin painfully, a reaction he wasn't going to be able to do a damn thing about and therefore had better ignore as best he could. Sawyer set his back teeth, so great was the effort it took to change the course of his thoughts. Altering the path of a river probably would have been easier, he soon concluded.

He willed himself to relax, one muscle group at a time, starting with the part of his anatomy in the most need of quieting, and when he'd finished, still taut and achy in too many places, he resorted to counting in his head, by odd numbers. After a while, as the imagined digits mounted to astronomical totals, he found he could breathe normally again. Some people prayed, and some people counted sheep, but Sawyer always took refuge in arithmetic.

He closed his eyes, hoping to sleep.

It was no use, though. He was too aware

of Piper, lying close by, in her spinsterish nightgown, with her glowing, just-bathed skin, and her dark hair clinging to her cheeks and forehead in moist tendrils. The scent of her was like perfume, faintly flowery, subtle.

"Mr. McKettrick?" Her voice was tentative. Soft. "Are you awake?"

He smiled again, having suspected she was playing possum. She'd called him by his given name once or twice that day, but now that they were both bedded down in the same room, "Mr. McKettrick" probably seemed a more prudent way to address him. "I'm awake," he confirmed.

He heard her draw in a breath. "I was just wondering if—well, if you think the man who shot you might come back?"

Bless her prim little heart, she was scared.

"Not likely," Sawyer said.

"Why not?"

"Because he probably thinks he's already killed me. Anyway, Blue River is small and a stranger would stand out."

"That didn't stop him before," she reasoned. "He just rode right up and shot you, bold as you please."

Sawyer grinned harder. His shoulder hurt, and he was lying a few feet from a woman he wanted and couldn't have, but he was enjoying this exchange. Maybe, he speculated, Miss Piper St. James was scared enough to leave her bed and share his.

"Yep," he said. "That's what happened."

"Suppose he didn't leave Blue River at all? Because of the storm, I mean. He could be holed up around here somewhere, couldn't he? Just waiting for his chance to strike again?"

"Maybe," Sawyer allowed, relishing her concern. If it hadn't meant Piper and her charges could be caught in the crossfire, he might have welcomed such a confrontation, since he'd be able to return the favor and put a bullet in the bastard, thereby evening the score. "It's not likely, though."

"What makes you so sure?"

"I've had some experience with these things," he replied.

"*That* isn't much comfort," Piper said. "Are you saying that you've been shot before?"

He had to chuckle. "No," he said. "I was referring to the nature of my work, that's all."

"What kind of 'work' involves getting shot?"

Sawyer said nothing.

"Are you an outlaw, Mr. McKettrick?" Piper persisted.

"Would you believe me if I said I wasn't?"

She made a muffled sound, like a scream of anger, held captive in her throat. It made him smile again. "I think you owe me an answer," she said, after a few moments.

"You do, do you?" he teased.

"Are you an outlaw?"

He thought it over. He'd killed a man once, though he'd been defending Henry Vandenburg, his former employer, at the time. Vandenburg's attacker, one of those wild-eyed anarchist types, had shoved his way through a crowd, in a busy railway station, and thrust the business end of a gun barrel into the boss's ample belly. Sawyer had stepped in, there was a struggle, and the pistol went off. The would-be killer bled out on the floor before the municipal police arrived in their paddy wagons.

"No," he answered, feigning offense at the question. "Would Clay have asked me to serve as town marshal if I were?"

"Possibly," she replied, after some thought. "You're his cousin, and the two of you grew up together. It might be that he's just giving you the benefit of the doubt by assuming that you are still the person he knew as a boy."

"Could be," Sawyer said, amused. She hadn't been this talkative before, and he wondered if that meant anything. Then he decided she felt safer speaking her mind because they were under cover of darkness, and she couldn't see him, or he her.

In a way, it reminded him of the old days on the Triple M, when he and Clay used to spend the night at their grandparents' house sometimes. The room they'd shared had two beds in it, and the dark of a country night had been like a curtain between them, making it possible to tell each other things they'd have choked on in the daylight.

"That," Piper said, "is a most unsatisfactory answer."

"Clay trusts me because I've never given him any reason not to," Sawyer said, relenting. Now that he wasn't in Vandenburg's employ any longer, he figured he didn't have to be so secretive, but he still wasn't inclined to spill his whole history. "I'm not an outlaw," he added.

"Then what are you? Only outlaws carry guns."

"Clay carries one. Is he an outlaw?"

"Well, *no,*" Piper admitted. "But he's the marshal."

There was a silence.

He waited.

"Are you a lawman?" she asked.

"Not exactly," Sawyer replied. He wondered if she'd warmed up yet, and if she was still scared—in need of a little manly protection. Being nobody's fool, he didn't ask. "How did you become acquainted with a lady of the evening?" he inquired instead, recalling that morning's visit from Bess Turner.

Piper sounded impatient. "You heard what she said—her daughter, Ginny-Sue, is one of my pupils. And if you're 'not exactly' a lawman, what are you?"

"I was paid to protect a man and his family," Sawyer said. "And that's all you need to know." He barely paused before giving her a dose of her own medicine by barging right into her private business. "Generally, respectable women don't befriend people like Ginny-Sue's mother, no matter what the circumstances."

Her tone was huffy. "Maybe I'm not a respectable woman. Did you ever think of that?"

Sawyer laughed. "Oh, you're respectable, all right. You wouldn't be so worried about my seeing you in a nightgown, not to mention our sharing a bedroom, if you weren't."

Piper was quiet for so long that Sawyer began to think she'd fallen asleep. Finally, though, she spoke again, and there was a note of gentle sorrow in her voice. "Bess loves her child, just like anybody else, and besides, however misguided she might be, she's a human being. I see no earthly reason to shun her."

Something thickened in Sawyer's throat, which was odd. He wasn't usually sentimental, especially not over prostitutes like Bess Turner, but something about Piper's offhand compassion touched him in a deep place, and caused a shift in the way he thought of her.

The realization caused him considerable consternation.

"Sawyer?"

He smiled at Piper's use of his first name. That was more like it. "What?"

"I'm—afraid."

"Don't be. I won't hurt you."

"It's not you I'm scared of. It's the man who shot you."

"In that case," he said, only half joking, "maybe you'd better crawl in with me."

"I couldn't do that!"

"Where's the harm in it? Your reputation is probably ruined anyhow."

There was a snap of irritation in her reply. "Be that as it may, I don't want to give you the wrong impression. I am *not* the sort of woman who gets into bed with a man she isn't married to." She swallowed so hard that he heard it. "I'm—unbesmirched."

Unbesmirched.

In other words, a virgin. No real surprise there.

"I won't lay a hand on you, Miss St. James," he assured her. That much was certainly true. He might *want* to do plenty, once Piper was lying beside him in that narrow bed, but he'd never tried to persuade an unwilling woman to share her favors before and he wasn't going to start now.

To his amazement, he heard her get out of the other bed, hurry over, and slip in beside him. The mattress was more suited to one than two; they collided, and Piper almost sprang out of bed again when she realized he wasn't wearing anything but the bandages and the sling on his left arm.

He knew this by the gasp she gave.

"It's *all right,* Piper," he said.

She gave a comical little wail. "You might have told me you were—well—*indisposed!*"

"You didn't ask," he pointed out.

"This is horrible," she lamented. But she was still there, under the covers. With him.

"Hardly," he said. "We're just two people keeping each other warm on a cold winter's night, that's all."

"Maybe that's all it is to *you,*" Piper retorted. "I had hopes of getting married someday, and having a home and a family, before you came along and spoiled everything."

He smiled in the darkness. "If that's so, then I'm sorry," he told her.

"You don't *sound* sorry," Piper accused.

He yawned expansively. "Would you be

convinced if I rounded up a preacher and the two of us got hitched?"

She gasped again.

He laughed, but the idea of taking a wife—*this* wife—was already starting to grow on him. He'd have preferred to court Piper St. James properly before he put a ring on her finger and took her home to the Triple M and the rest of the McKettrick family, but she had a point. Whether it was fair or not, she was probably compromised, all right, simply because they'd been alone together for a couple of days and nights. Some folks were just hypocritical enough to assume she'd thrown caution to the winds and succumbed to rampant lust at the first opportunity.

It was downright ridiculous, Sawyer knew, to assume a conscientious schoolmarm would turn into a raving wanton overnight, since she'd given shelter to a wounded stranger of the opposite sex, and never mind the kindness and courage she'd shown by dragging him inside and looking after him as best she knew how. After this, Piper would be no better than Bess Turner, as far as a lot of the locals were concerned.

Piper hadn't answered his question and now, judging by the moisture he felt against the upper part of his right arm, she was in tears.

"Hey," he said hoarsely, "don't cry."

"I can't help it," she sobbed. Since he reckoned she wasn't the kind who cried easily, this was even worse. "Isn't it enough that you *ruined my life?* Do you have to add insult to injury by *mocking* me, too?"

Sawyer was honestly confused. "Mocking you?" he rasped. God, he hated it when women cried, especially when it was his fault. Like now. "When did I do that?"

"When you m-made that r-remark about getting—hitched!"

"Piper," he said, surprising himself as he much as he had her, "I was serious. I'll marry you, if it'll make you feel better."

She struggled to a sitting position, and moonlight turned her tears silvery on her cheeks. Her hair fell loose around her shoulders and down her back, nearly reaching her waist. "But we don't *love* each other!" she cried, in obvious despair.

Gently, he drew Piper back down beside him, holding her with his good arm. She rested her head on his bare shoulder, sniffling. "That's true," he said carefully, "but we certainly wouldn't be the first couple who ever got married for practical reasons. Clay and Dara Rose tied the knot so she and the girls would have a place to live, and that arrangement worked out."

Instead of comforting her, Sawyer's words made her cry harder.

He was confounded, figuring he'd made a good case for holy matrimony.

He patted the back of her head ineffectually, afraid to say anything more in case he got it wrong. Again.

"That's different!" Piper wailed out, after some shuddering and sniffling.

"What's different?" Sawyer asked carefully.

"Clay and Dara Rose are different!"

"Why?"

"Because they were in love with each other from the very first," Piper sobbed. "It just took them a while to notice!"

Against his better judgment, Sawyer laughed. He couldn't help it. "People get married for all sorts of reasons," he reiterated, when he'd caught his breath. "Love isn't always one of them."

"Well, it should be!"

"Lots of things 'should be,' but they aren't." It was the wrong thing to say, but Sawyer didn't realize that until after he'd said it, when she slammed the side of one small fist into his belly. The blow didn't hurt, but it sure startled him, and it knocked the wind out of him for a moment, too.

Piper might be small, but she packed a punch. Raised by and around strong women, Sawyer considered that a good thing.

"I don't even know what kind of man you are," she lamented, though she seemed to be regaining some control of her runaway emotions. "You could be a scoundrel, or worse."

He smiled. "What's worse?" he teased. A strand of her hair tickled his mouth, and he decided he liked the feeling.

"Murder," she said. "Highway robbery. *Bigamy.*"

"Bigamy?"

"Dara Rose thought she was married to Edrina and Harriet's father," Piper blurted out, on one long breath, "and it turned out he already had a wife and children, that stinker!"

Sawyer remembered Clay telling him

the story, the year before. He hadn't thought about it since, though. "I'm not married," he said quietly. "Never have been."

She sat up again, looking down at him. "How do I know you're telling the truth?"

Was she considering saying yes?

"You don't," he said solemnly. "You'll just have to trust me."

She ruminated on that for a while, still sitting up. "You didn't—you couldn't have— *meant* what you said? About us getting married?"

"I meant it, all right," Sawyer replied. He actually *liked* the idea, and that was a bit unsettling.

"If we go through with this, it would be a marriage in name only."

Up until now, Sawyer couldn't have imagined himself agreeing to such terms, but he did. "All right," he said. "But I reserve the right to try to change your mind."

Piper mulled that over. He reckoned she was going to come to her senses and pull out of the deal. "Not until *after* we're married," she negotiated.

"Fair enough," Sawyer said, and something inside him soared, as proud and free as a lone eagle against a wide blue sky. "Can I at least kiss you?"

More consideration on her part followed.

He sat up, careful to keep the quilts in place, just above his waist.

They stared at each other for a while, in the light of a waning moon filtering through a weather-grimed window.

Then she closed her eyes, puckered up, and waited.

Sawyer bit the inside of his lower lip, so he wouldn't laugh. Then he placed his hand on the back of her head, very gently, and pressed her face toward his. He kissed her, worked her lips with his own until Piper sighed and opened to him.

He used his tongue. Carefully.

She moaned and slipped her arms around his neck.

He deepened the kiss slowly, because she was so obviously an innocent.

Piper whimpered, but she didn't try to pull away.

It was Sawyer who did that. "Piper," he said, his voice ragged from the strain of giving up what the rest of his body was demanding, "no more. I'm trying to do the right thing here."

"I'd better go back to the other bed," she said shyly.

"That might be a good idea," Sawyer replied. He was hard as tamarack by then, and he didn't want Piper to know it.

She left him, got back into the bed Clay had brought in from the ranch. The small distance between them seemed like miles to Sawyer, who fell back onto his pillows with a heavy sigh.

"Sawyer?" Piper said.

He probably sounded abrupt when he replied. "What?"

"I've never—" She fell silent, embarrassed again.

"I know," he said more gently.

And after that, by some miracle, they both went to sleep.

PIPER'S EYES FLEW open when she realized it was morning, and she'd not only let Sawyer kiss her in the night, but she'd kissed him *back.* She sat up in her borrowed bed, pulling the covers up to her chin, and looked in his direction, but he wasn't there.

She scrambled out from under the blankets, landed both feet on the icy floor, and made a dash for her bureau, where she rummaged for bloomers and a camisole. Clutching them in one hand, she grabbed her woolen dress, the one she'd planned on saving for really cold days, and stuck her head out the bedroom door.

Sawyer wasn't in the schoolroom—he must have gcne outside, to the privy.

Piper dressed in seconds, fumbling, hopping about, nearly tripping over her hem in the process, and then did what she could with her hair, winding it into a single plait and twisting it around the back of her head, where she secured it with hairpins.

The schoolroom was warm—Sawyer must have built up the fire—and the delicious aroma of fresh coffee filled the air. She went to the window, looked out. The snow was nearly gone, but she barely took note of that because she spotted Sawyer, dressed and talking amiably with Doc Howard, who didn't get down off his mule. The poor animal was muddy to its knees.

Piper saw Doc smile and nod his head, and she ducked back from the window quickly, hoping he hadn't seen her.

What was Sawyer *saying* out there?

Her cheeks flamed so hot that she pressed her palms to her face, trying to cool them down. *Surely* Sawyer wasn't asking Doc Howard to fetch a preacher, so he and the schoolmarm could "get hitched," she thought frantically. Yes, they'd talked about marriage, and it had seemed like a viable idea at the time, but in the bright light of day it was—well, it was insane, that's what it was. It was *out of the question.*

She remembered the kiss, felt the heat and pressure on her mouth as surely as if Sawyer's mouth was on hers right then.

Her heart pounded, and bolts of fiery lightning shot through her, weakening her knees, melting parts of her that were too personal even to *think about.*

She *was* wanton, she concluded, horrified. She'd not only *gotten into bed* with Sawyer McKettrick the night before, she'd let him kiss her. *Let* him? She'd as good as thrown herself at the man, and then she'd *carried on.* In fact, if Sawyer hadn't sent her back to her own bed, she might have been swept away.

Things, she decided, could not possibly get worse.

Except that they did, and almost immediately.

Sawyer opened the door, came inside, spotted her sitting on one of her students' desks with her hands pressed to her burning face.

He smiled. "There are some kids coming down the road," he informed her. "Your students, I presume."

Piper cried out, bolted to her feet. "No!"

"Yes," Sawyer said. "Doc will be back at three-thirty, with a license and a preacher." With that, he headed for the bedroom, pausing to pour himself a mug full of coffee along the way. From the inside doorway, he looked back at her over his right shoulder. "Better step lively, Teacher," he said. "School's about to be in session."

He was barely out of sight when Ginny-Sue Turner burst in, cheeks pink, eyes eager. "I know the whole second chapter of Luke!" she blurted joyfully. "By heart!"

Piper's smile might have been a little shaky, but Ginny-Sue was too young, and too excited, to notice. "That's wonderful," she said, resting a hand on the child's shoulder.

"And Christmas is going to happen, after all!" Ginny-Sue enthused, glowing as she got out of her coat and mittens and warm woolen hat. "Mama said it would, because you told her so."

Piper's throat tightened, and she managed a little nod. She had no power to keep another snowstorm away, of course, but this child clearly believed she did.

It was a weighty responsibility.

Madeline Howard arrived next, small and blonde and very pretty, like her mother, followed by half a dozen other children.

"May I ring the bell, Miss St. James?" Madeline asked, beaming.

Piper assented, and the other students arrived by twos and threes. Even Edrina and Harriet made it into town for class— Clay had driven them in a wagon drawn by those same two plow horses he'd hitched to the sledge the day before, and he waved and smiled from the seat, reins in hand.

"Has the baby arrived?" Piper asked breathlessly, after picking her way through the mud to stand beside Clay's wagon, looking up at him.

He shook his head. "Not yet," he said, "but Dara Rose was mighty eager to get the girls out of the house this morning, so I figure she's about ready."

"You'd better get back there, quick,"

Piper said, worried, but thrilled, too. In her excitement, she forgot about Sawyer Mc-Kettrick, hiding out in her bedroom behind the schoolhouse.

He'd be discovered, of course, if only because Edrina and Harriet surely knew he was there, and would want to greet him.

Clay nodded, lifted the reins and released the brake lever with his left hand. "Sawyer doing all right?" he asked, in parting.

Piper colored up, quite against her will, but held Clay's gaze. "Yes," she said.

Clay touched the brim of his hat in farewell, brought down the reins on the horses' backs, setting them in noisy motion, and drove away.

If it hadn't been so cold outside, sunny sky or none, Piper might have lingered in the schoolyard, putting off the moment when she'd have to face her pupils, but she didn't have a cloak and she'd forgotten to wrap the blanket around her before coming to greet Clay.

So she marched inside, clapping her hands to get the children's attention.

They were gathered around the undecorated Christmas tree, examining it for bird's nests and chatting among themselves. Edrina and Harriet, as she'd expected, were out of sight, and she could hear them talking with Sawyer in the back room.

She closed her eyes for a moment.

"Can we fix up the Christmas tree today, Miss St. James?" one of the boys asked. "Jack and me, we could fix up a stand for it in no time, out in the woodshed."

Piper set her hands on her hips and considered the suggestion in a teacherly way. "That would be fine," she said, at long last.

The children cheered.

Two of the boys rushed outside, followed by several more.

"Edrina, Harriet!" Piper called pleasantly. "Come out here, please. We're going to decorate the tree."

Dara Rose's children, both beautiful, with heads full of shining curls and cherubic faces, appeared in the bedroom doorway.

Harriet opened her little bow-shaped mouth, most likely on the verge of making some remark about her kinsman's presence, but Piper quickly pressed an index finger to her own lips, shushing her.

Though she was very young, only in the first grade, Harriet read Piper's signal and bit back whatever she'd planned to say.

For the next hour, the children kept busy, cutting strips of colorful paper, saved especially for the purpose, and pasting them together in loops, so they turned into long chains.

The boys returned from the shed, triumphant, with several pieces of wood cobbled together to serve as a stand for the tree.

After much ado, the stem of the tree was wedged into the simple stand. Piper found the box of handmade ornaments on the cloakroom shelf and brought it into the schoolroom, where the lid was ceremoniously raised.

Inside were other chains, made by other students and other teachers, along with a few carefully wrapped glass balls, tiny ragdoll angels, and stars cut from tin. Some of the stars had rusted, which only added to their charm, and the children were as enthralled as if they'd just found a pirate's treasure.

Soon, the tree stood glittering, ready for Christmas.

By midday, the weather was turning gloomy again, the sky dark and heavy with snow, and fathers and uncles arrived in wagons and on horseback, to collect their offspring and see them safely home. Two of the mothers came as well, and peered curiously at Piper, as though they weren't sure they recognized her.

When the first fat snowflakes drifted down, Ginny-Sue took her leave, squeezing Piper's hand before she hurried outside. "Don't worry, Teacher," she said.

"Christmas will still come—you'll see!"

CHAPTER 6

Of all Piper's pupils, only Edrina and Harriet remained at the schoolhouse, waiting for Clay to come for them. Heedless of the continuing snow, they laughed with Sawyer, who had hauled Piper's rocking chair out of the bedroom and now sat with one of the little girls on each knee, telling stories about himself and Clay as boys.

The fire in the stove warmed the room and steamed up the windows in a cozy way, and the Christmas tree lent a definite air of festivity, but Piper was nervous, just the same.

From a practical standpoint, she knew

that Clay wasn't late—it was not quite three o'clock and he had farther to travel than most of the other parents—and even if he'd gotten off to an early start, the weather would surely slow him down.

No, it was Dara Rose she was concerned about.

Hadn't Clay said, that very morning, that Dara Rose had seemed anxious to get her daughters out of the house? Wasn't that an indication that the baby might be coming?

Piper bit her lower lip and busied herself at her desk, pretending to study her attendance records. Dara Rose was healthy, she reminded herself, and strong. She'd had two other children with no problem at all, hadn't she?

But Edrina and Harriet had been born in a large *city*, with a real doctor present at each of their births, and Dara Rose had been younger then.

Was she giving birth right now, this minute, way out there on that isolated ranch?

Had she run into some kind of trouble with the delivery, the kind Clay didn't have the knowledge or skill to handle?

At three-fifteen Piper heard the squeal of wagon wheels being braked, the snorting and tromping of horses, and rushed to the front window to wipe away some of the mist and look outside.

Clay, wearing a heavy coat, with the brim of his hat pulled low over his eyes to shield his face from the blustery weather, jumped down from the wagon box and left the team standing, their nostrils puffing out white clouds of breath.

Piper looked harder, trying to discern something from Clay's bearing or manner—his face was still hidden from view by the angle of his hat—but he revealed nothing as he made his way toward the schoolhouse with long, even strides.

Edrina and Harriet must have heard the team and wagon, too, because they were beside Piper in a matter of moments, standing on tiptoe, fingers gripping the windowsill, trying to see out. Perhaps they'd been more anxious than they'd let on.

Clay finally reached the porch, paused to stomp the snow and mud from his boots.

Piper wrenched open the door, but stepped aside when Edrina and Harriet scrambled past her.

Clay stepped over the threshold, shut the door, and crouched, putting out an arm for each of the girls. His hat fell backward and the beaming smile on his face was revealed.

"Girls," he told his stepdaughters, his eyes misting over like the windows, "you've got a brand-new baby brother waiting for you out at the ranch. Your mama's just fine, and she's hankering to show the little fellow off to you."

Edrina and Harriet jumped up and down with happiness as Clay straightened, nodded a brief greeting to Sawyer, then shifted his gaze to Piper.

"It was an easy birth," he told her quietly. "Dara Rose is well, if a mite worn-out, and the baby is big enough to fight bear with a switch."

Piper wept tears of joyful relief and gave Clay a quick, sisterly hug.

"Congratulations," she said, stepping back and smiling up at him.

That was when she felt Sawyer standing behind her. He rested his good hand on her shoulder briefly before reaching past her to extend it to Clay.

The two men shook hands.

"Another McKettrick," Sawyer said. "I'm not sure the world is ready for that."

Clay laughed. His face and ears were red with cold, but his eyes gleamed with love and pride. "We're going to call him Jeb," he said, "after my pa."

"Will you stay for coffee?" Piper asked, out of practicality. "It'll help keep you warm on the way back home."

But Clay shook his head in refusal, nodded to the girls to get their things together so the three of them could get going. "If we hurry, we can make it before dark," he said, more to Piper and Sawyer than the children, who were busy bundling up for the long, chilly ride ahead. "Dara Rose will fret if we're not back in time for supper."

Piper felt tearful again, full of longing. Oh, to go with Clay and Edrina and Harriet, to make supper for the family and fuss over Dara Rose and the new baby.

Clay seemed to read her mind. "It'll be Christmas soon," he said, gruffly gentle. "You'll see Dara Rose and make Jeb's acquaintance then."

She swallowed, nodded, and hastened to help Edrina and Harriet with their coats and hats and mittens and scarves. She kissed each one of them goodbye—when the other pupils were around she tried hard not to show favoritism—and said she'd see them in the morning, if the weather allowed.

"You need anything?" Clay asked as an afterthought, glancing at Piper but mainly addressing Sawyer, after he'd put on his hat and sent the girls racing for the wagon out front.

"No," Sawyer said, with warmth and amusement in his voice. "You go on home and look after your family, cousin. We'll be just fine on our own."

Inwardly, Piper stiffened. In all the excitement over the new baby, she'd forgotten all about Doc's imminent return, with the preacher in tow.

No sense bringing that up in front of Clay, though. It would take too much explaining, and he might feel torn between going home to Dara Rose and the baby and staying for the wedding.

Not that there was going to *be* a wedding.

Piper meant to make that abundantly

clear as soon as she and Sawyer were alone. She'd made a rash decision, she'd tell him, but now she'd changed her mind.

Only when Clay and the girls drove away did she turn around to face Sawyer.

He was standing so close that his injured arm, still in its sling, bumped against her breast. A slow, sultry smile lit his eyes and touched his mouth. *That* mouth. Piper could almost feel it against her own, seeking, exploring, and finally, commanding.

She caught her own breath. "About last night—"

Sawyer grinned, easy in his skin and damnably sure of himself, and curled his right index finger under her chin. "A deal's a deal, Miss St. James," he told her huskily. "Besides, the word's surely out by now. There's a man over at the schoolhouse, that's what folks are saying, and something unseemly is going on for sure."

Piper pressed her back teeth together. He was right, of course. She'd seen the way those mothers, those *hens*, had looked at her, when they came to gather their chicks under their figurative wings. They'd known, even before their children got a chance to give an account. Eloise Howard must have spread the word, just as Piper had feared she would.

Besides, the Blue River schoolhouse was too small to contain such a secret; even though Sawyer had been courteous enough to stay out of sight while the students were there, they would have guessed that Edrina and Harriet weren't addressing empty space when they'd hurried into the back room that morning, chattering like happy little magpies. Why, they hadn't even paused to take off their coats.

Piper gave a little groan of frustration. "What if we're making a terrible mistake?" she whispered hoarsely.

Sawyer smiled, placed a brief, feather-soft kiss on her mouth, instantly awakening every wanton tendency she possessed— and the number of those tendencies was alarming.

"Most of your questions start with 'what if' or 'how do I know,'" he observed. "There aren't any guarantees in this life, Piper. The whole proposition is risky from the get-go right up to the end." He paused, wound a finger idly in a tendril of her hair, a gesture almost as intimate as last night's kiss. "I can promise you this much, though—I'll provide for you, I'll protect you, and I'll never lay a hand on you except to give you pleasure."

Pleasure? She blinked at the word. She'd always considered that the province of men and, perhaps, women like Bess Turner.

But, wait, she reflected, avoiding Sawyer's eyes by looking down and to the side. Dara Rose wasn't a loose woman, and she certainly seemed to enjoy married life. She hadn't said so outright, but Piper *had* wondered, a time or two, about the way her cousin and Clay smiled secrets at each other. The way they touched when they thought no one was looking.

Sawyer touched the tip of her nose just then, and her gaze swung straight to his, connected with a jolt, like a metal latch. "You're blushing," he said, in a low, pleased drawl. "Was it the word *pleasure?*"

"Of course not," Piper lied. She'd been raised, like most women of her generation, to believe that "pleasure" and "wickedness" were one and the same thing. Luckily, she was saved from having to make a case for propriety by a knock at the door.

She jumped at the sound, startled because she hadn't heard a wagon or a horse approaching the schoolhouse.

Sawyer merely smiled.

She whirled away from him, in a billow of gray skirts, and opened the door, thinking Clay and the girls must have found the going too hard and turned back. Nothing would have stopped Clay from returning to Dara Rose and the baby, she knew, but that didn't mean he'd put Edrina and Harriet's safety at risk in the doing of it. He'd leave them with her, if he thought they were in any danger.

Instead of Clay and the girls, though, she found herself face-to-face with Doc Howard, his smugly disapproving wife, Eloise, and the Methodist circuit preacher, a towering, bearded man of dour countenance, fearsome as an Old Testament prophet bringing word of impending doom. He looked ready for battle, too, as though he'd come to that little schoolhouse to fight the devil himself, hand to hand, standing there with snow dusting the shoulders of his tattered coat and the brim of his once-fine hat.

"C-come in," Piper said, stepping back

to admit them all. She was only too aware of Sawyer standing nearby, looking on with amusement.

Blast him, he was *enjoying* this, she just knew it.

"You've made a wise decision," Mrs. Howard said loftily, pulling off her elbow-length kid gloves and narrowing her eyes at Piper as she spoke. She wore a dark blue woolen cloak over a dress almost the same color, and her hat was huge. With the snow, it looked as though the woman was carrying a miniature landscape on her head.

Dislike welled up in Piper, but she held it in check. She was, regrettably, in no position to make her opinions known, especially since Mrs. Howard was on the school board and could have her dismissed without any difficulty at all.

"Have I?" Piper countered, with false sweetness.

Eloise Howard narrowed her china-blue eyes even further, to little lash-trimmed slits. Doc Howard, the preacher, and even Sawyer seemed to recede into the now-fuzzy surroundings. "I'm sure you'll agree, *Miss* St. James," Eloise said, through her tiny, perfect teeth, "that the moral well-being of our children must be the paramount consideration here."

Piper was mad enough to spit. She was a good teacher and, besides, it wasn't as if she'd been teaching her pupils to dance the hurdy-gurdy. This situation, meaning Sawyer's presence at the schoolhouse, had *befallen* her—she'd done nothing to bring it about, nothing at all.

Except for trying to do the right thing.

She was to be held accountable, nonetheless, and that, in her opinion, was a travesty.

"Now, Eloise," Doc interceded, after clearing his throat, "leave the preaching to Brother Carson, here."

Nobody laughed at the paltry joke, if it was intended as one, or even smiled.

No one besides Sawyer, that is. Out of the corner of her eye, Piper saw the corner of his mouth twitch.

"Morality is a serious matter," Brother Carson pontificated, in a thundering voice. He held a huge Bible in the crook of one arm, as though poised to use it as a weapon if the need presented itself. His gaze sliced, lethal and dark with condemnation, between Sawyer and Piper. "God is not mocked," he added. "We must root out sin wherever we find it!"

Piper didn't know how to respond to that, except to flinch slightly and take half a step backward, which caused her to collide with Sawyer.

Determinedly jovial, Doc Howard chose that moment to shove a parcel at Sawyer— it was wrapped in brown paper and tied with string. "Here are the things you asked me to fetch from the general store," he said, a little too loudly. Then, spotting the Christmas tree, he went on, "Now isn't that a merry sight!"

"We can thank the Germans for that bit of frippery," the preacher boomed, without appreciation. "A fire hazard at best, idolatry at worst."

"What's this world coming to?" Sawyer mused lightly.

Piper resisted the temptation to elbow him, hard. She couldn't take a chance on doing further injury to his bad shoulder.

Eloise was still watching her, with a sort of curious abhorrence, the way she might watch some poor soul traveling with a freak show, but she directed her words to her husband when she spoke. "What about the marriage license, James?" she asked, in a condescending tone. "Did you 'fetch' one of those, too?"

Doc Howard blushed slightly, and Piper felt sorry for him.

Her own dealings with Eloise Howard were intermittent ones. His were constant.

He patted the front of his suit coat, then reached into the inside pocket and drew out a folded document. "It's right here," he said. "Judge Reynolds agreed that this is an emergency, so he issued the license without the usual waiting period."

Brother Carson opened his Bible, flipped through the pages until he found a sheet of paper tucked away in the Psalms, and cleared his throat. "Dearly beloved," he growled out, squinting down at the words scrawled in black ink, "we are gathered here—in the sight of God—"

"Wait," Piper interrupted, but after that, words deserted her.

Brother Carson looked up, his black eyebrows bushy as caterpillars.

Eloise Howard blinked once.

"I know this must seem hasty," Doc put in bravely, after an anxious glance at his wife, "but there's nothing for it. Marriage is the only solution."

"But—" Piper protested.

Sawyer cupped a hand under her elbow just then, and, somehow, that gave her strength. They were being railroaded into this, both she and Sawyer, but she supposed the situation could have been worse.

He might have been old and ugly, for instance.

And she might have been repulsed, rather than excited, by his kisses.

She sighed. "Go ahead," she said wearily.

And so it happened that Piper St. James was married—*married*—to a man she barely knew. Instead of a wedding gown, she wore her gray woolen schoolmarm's dress. There were no real guests, no family members present; she didn't even have a bridal bouquet.

The whole ceremony was over in under ten minutes, in fact.

Piper was in such a daze that she barely registered Sawyer's perfunctory wedding kiss.

They each signed the marriage license,

and Doc snatched it up like it was a Spanish land grant or something, saying he'd file it with Judge Reynolds and bring back a copy when he could.

The preacher slammed his Bible shut on his handwritten wedding vows, nodded abruptly, and turned to leave without so much as a goodbye.

Doc, too, seemed anxious to escape, and he all but dragged Eloise out of the schoolhouse. Mrs. Howard, Piper suspected, with rancor, would have preferred to stay and gloat for a few minutes.

In what seemed like a blink of an eye, the others were gone, leaving Piper alone with her new husband.

She squeezed her eyes shut, willing herself not to cry.

The rustle of paper caught her attention, and she looked sideways to see that Sawyer was opening the parcel Doc had given him earlier. He'd set it aside, without comment, in order to make his marriage vows.

A garment made of rich, russet-colored wool lay folded inside, along with a narrow gold wedding band, perched atop one of the folds.

Smiling, Sawyer slipped the band onto her finger.

Amazingly, it was a perfect fit, like Cinderella's glass slipper in the fairy tale.

Piper couldn't speak. Moments before, she'd been on the verge of tears, and now she wanted to laugh like a madwoman. She was hysterical, that was it.

And, furthermore, she was *Mrs. McKettrick.*

Who *was* that, exactly? How was she to proceed?

Using his right hand, Sawyer caressed her cheek. "I'll keep my word, Piper," he said. "For now, we're only married on paper."

Her eyes widened. "For now?" she echoed. Surely this was all a dream—a terrible, wonderful dream—and she'd awaken at any moment.

Again, that wicked tilt appeared at the corner of his mouth. "I have every intention of seducing you," he said, his voice at once quiet and forthright, "sooner or later. In the meantime, you're a respectable woman again."

Piper might have taken umbrage at that, if he hadn't chosen that moment to unfurl the beautiful russet-colored cape he'd bought for her. It had a deep, elegant hood and was trimmed in black silk piping.

She'd seen the garment on display over at the mercantile, not once but many times, but it cost the earth and she'd never given a single thought to owning it. Neither had most of the other women in town, she'd bet, since it was the sort of thing a grand lady would wear to the opera.

Needless to say, there was no opera in Blue River, Texas.

Spellbound, she accepted the cloak, draping it around her shoulders, marveling at the weight of it, and the supple softness of the fabric, almost like velvet, and the way it seemed to wrap her in grace.

"Do you like it?" Sawyer asked. He sounded almost shy. "I guess it wouldn't have been a proper gift before, but now that we're married—"

She raised shining eyes to him. "Oh, Sawyer," she said, in a rapt whisper. "I've never seen anything so beautiful."

"Neither have I," he said then, very gravely.

And he was looking at her as he spoke, not at the cloak.

Piper's native practicality reasserted itself a few moments later, and she took the
cape to the cloakroom and hung it up there,
out of the way, where it wouldn't be stained,
or get snagged on something.

"Thank you," she said, with crisp dignity,
when she came out again.

Sawyer was feeding wood into the stove
by then. "You're welcome," he said.

Shyness overwhelmed Piper in that
moment. She didn't know how to be this
new person, this Mrs. McKettrick she'd
become with almost no warning at all. "You
were forced into this," she murmured. "Just
as I was. It isn't fair."

"I guess we're victims of circumstance,"
Sawyer replied philosophically. "Nothing
to do now but make the best of things."

"I'll start supper," Piper said quickly, maintaining a safe distance. It wasn't that she
didn't trust Sawyer, exactly; if he were a
masher, she'd have known it by now. Even
with one arm bound up in a sling, he could
have taken advantage of her at almost any
point in their brief acquaintance.

No, she realized, it was *herself* she didn't
completely trust.

She'd gotten into bed with this man the night before.

She'd allowed him to kiss her—not only allowed it, but *reveled* in it.

It made her blush to think what she might have let Sawyer do after that, if he hadn't had the decency to send her away.

The truth struck her, hard.

Even the forced marriage hadn't been entirely beyond her control—she could have packed a satchel, boarded a train and left Blue River forever, started over somewhere else, maybe even changed her name. Or she could have put her foot down, that very afternoon, when the Howards and Brother Carson showed up, and flatly refused to go through with the ceremony.

There would have been repercussions, of course. But wasn't being married to a man she barely *knew* a repercussion?

There was no getting around it. Some part of her had *wanted* this, had seen the chance and reached out to grab hold.

Piper was baffled by all this, even stricken, and yet—excited, even thrilled. Her life had always been so proper, so predictable, so *ordinary.*

Now, all of a sudden, some other, unknown Piper had come to the fore and quite handily taken matters into her own hands. This was a bold and brazen Piper, a person she'd never imagined she could be.

Leaving her to her confusion, probably blithely unaware of it, being a man, Sawyer went outside for wood and water, managing these chores ably with one arm, and it struck Piper that he was recovering rapidly. He still needed a shave, but his hair was combed and his color was good, and he seemed to have significantly more stamina than one might have expected, after such a severe and recent injury.

Soon, he'd be well enough to leave the schoolhouse.

Maybe he'd even change his mind about accepting the marshal's job, and go back to his former occupation, whatever that was. He'd said he'd been paid to "protect a man and his family." Was that just a polite way of saying he was a common *henchman?* An outlaw, for all practical intents and purposes?

As for the marriage, well, that might have been some sort of ruse on his part.

Men walked out on wives and families all the time, didn't they?

Piper gave herself a mental shake as she sliced more of Dara Rose's ham and laid it in the skillet waiting on the stove. She was letting her imagination run away with her. If Sawyer already had a wife tucked away somewhere, *someone* in that sprawling McKettrick clan would know about her, wouldn't they? According to Dara Rose, Clay exchanged letters with half the family. Surely, he'd have heard the news from one of his many relations, if not Sawyer himself. And honor would have demanded that he step in and prevent an illegal marriage.

Except that Clay hadn't *known* she and Sawyer were about to get married. She hadn't had a chance to tell him, wouldn't have known what to say if she had, and it was a good bet that Sawyer hadn't said anything to his cousin, either.

Sawyer came in, bringing the scent of snow and pine pitch along with him, and dropped wood into the box next to the stove.

"I don't think this weather is going to last,"

he said. "The snow's melting as soon as it hits the ground."

Piper nodded, biting her lower lip and spearing at the slices of ham with a fork as though the task required all her concentration. This was her wedding night, she thought, with glum amazement, catching sight of the golden band shimmering on her finger.

How had this *happened*?

Just a few days ago, she'd been an ordinary schoolteacher, a little discontented with her lot in life, perhaps, but certainly not unhappy. Now, she was legally Mrs. Sawyer McKettrick—but what did that mean, exactly? Would she even be able to keep her job?

Married women rarely taught school—it was considered improper and a poor reflection on the husband's ability to provide—even if said husband was a worthless layabout, drinking his way to the grave. The wife and any children unfortunate enough to be born of such a union were expected to politely starve to death, without so much as a whimper of complaint, if only for the sake of appearances.

Appearances!

Piper forgot herself and swore aloud. "Thunderation!" she blurted out.

Sawyer reminded her of his presence with a question. "Did you burn yourself?" he asked, from somewhere behind her. He sounded calmly concerned.

"No," Piper said. "I was just thinking about—things."

"Things?"

"Men. Women. Marriage."

He eased her aside, took over the fork she'd been wielding, repeatedly turning the meat in the skillet, whether it needed turning or not. "I'll do this," he said. "And what about men, women and marriage?"

She flounced to her desk chair and plunked down in it, glad to have something to think about besides what might happen when the lamps went out later in the evening. She had no confidence whatsoever in her own ability to conduct herself like a lady.

"Women get a raw deal," she said. "We can't even *vote*, for pity's sake."

"I agree with you there," Sawyer replied, surprising her. "It isn't right."

Piper was picking up steam, like a locomotive chugging out of the station. "Men can go right ahead and beat women, if they want to, wives *and* children. If they're no-accounts, their wives can't go out and earn a living, even to put food on the table or keep a roof over their heads. They wind up like Bess Turner if they try."

"Whoa," Sawyer said affably, forking the meat onto two plates and bringing one to her, along with a slice of the bread she'd already sliced and buttered and a spoonful from the jar of peaches she'd opened the night before. "If that's what you think marriage is going to be like, it's no wonder you're jumpy."

Piper drew in a deep breath. "I might have gotten a little carried away," she admitted, touched that he'd brought her supper to her. Except for Clay, who doted on Dara Rose even though he was unquestionably the head of their family, she'd never seen a married man do that.

He went back for his own plate and sat on the edge of the desk to eat. "I wouldn't beat you," he said, after a long time. "Or any kids we might be lucky enough to have. For that matter, I wouldn't beat a dog or a horse or any other living creature."

She looked up at him. "Not even a man?" she asked.

"That's different," he said, his gaze level as he studied her.

"Is it?"

"Yes," Sawyer replied, after a few moments of thought. "I don't go around looking for fights, Piper, but if one comes my way, I mean to hold my own. And if I run into the yahoo who shot me, I'll shoot him without missing a breath."

"You are a very complicated man," she observed presently, having mulled over what he'd said.

He cocked a grin at her. "I reckon I am," he said. "Keeps things interesting, wouldn't you say?"

She sighed, let the question go unanswered, since she knew it didn't need a reply, and presented one of her own. "What happens when you're well, Sawyer?" she asked, with a glance at his sling and bandages, bulging under one side of his half-buttoned shirt. "Will you stay here in Blue River, and serve as marshal?" *Or will you retrieve your fancy horse from Clay's barn and ride out, leaving me behind?*

"I'll be here long enough to track down the son-of-a—the man who shot me, and make sure justice is served. Come spring, though, I expect to head north, home to the Triple M. Build a house and settle down."

In all that, there was no mention of bringing a wife along, but Piper didn't point out the omission. For one thing, she was much more concerned by Sawyer's implacability, and his plan to bring in his assailant.

He could get killed doing that.

Or become a killer.

Both possibilities terrified Piper.

They finished their suppers in silence, and Piper did the dishes—Sawyer tried to help, but she elbowed him aside.

Darkness gathered, thick, at the windows, and the little stove labored hard to keep out the evening chill, though the snow had stopped coming down, at least.

Sawyer rummaged around and found the battered checkerboard and chunky wooden game pieces Miss Krenshaw or one of her predecessors had left behind. Piper sometimes allowed the children to hold tournaments, on days when they'd behaved particularly well and completed their lessons to her satisfaction.

He set the board up on her desk. "Black or red?" he asked.

Piper, drying her hands, turned away from the dish basin, the task complete. "What?" she asked.

Sawyer grinned. "Do you want the red pieces, or the black ones?"

She frowned. "You want to play checkers?"

His grin widened. "There are things I'd rather do," he admitted, "this being our wedding night. But I'm a man of my word, Mrs. McKettrick. A virgin bride you are, and a virgin bride you will remain. For the time being, that is."

She blushed. "Red," she said.

He gestured toward her chair, and she sat down. He rested one hip on the other side of her desk, as he'd done before, when they were having supper.

"Your move," he said.

CHAPTER 7

This wasn't how she'd envisioned her wedding night, Piper reflected, as she and Sawyer played game after game of checkers, on the surface of her desk—which wasn't to say she'd ever had a clear idea of what was *supposed* to happen. Oh, she knew the fundamentals, of course, the strictly anatomical part, but the rest belonged to the realm of speculation—mostly. She *had* felt some very interesting sensations when Sawyer kissed her the night before, ones that made her want more of the same, but her fear equaled her curiosity, perhaps even exceeded it.

The congress between a man and a woman, she had been taught, mostly by inference and whispers, was mainly a nasty and painful business, something to be tolerated, endured, with the husband's happiness as a reward and, of course, the possible conception of a baby.

To Piper, the bearing, raising and cherishing of a child of her own—and preferably several—was a sacred calling indeed. Although she loved teaching, she knew the vocation was, at least for her, a prelude to mothering.

As for the husband . . . well, a good one, like Clay, was a blessing. A *bad* one, on the other hand, would be a curse. Which kind *she'd* gotten remained to be seen.

Keeping her gaze focused on her game pieces—she was losing, badly, *again*—Piper considered Dara Rose, and the way she lit up from the inside whenever Clay was around. She hummed a great deal, Piper had noticed on visits to the ranch, and even sang under her breath while she went about her household tasks. And even though there was never any overt sign of their intentions, Dara Rose didn't seem to dread being alone with her husband at night, behind a closed bedroom door.

The whole thing was downright confusing, and Piper wished she'd been bold enough to ask Dara Rose what marital relations were really like, in their most elemental form.

Sawyer knit his brow, and while his eyes smiled, his mouth played at a frown. "What's going on in your mind right about now, Mrs. McKettrick?" he asked.

She didn't protest the "Mrs. McKettrick" part, even though she thought it contained a trace of benign mockery. "Nothing I want to discuss with *you*, Mr. McKettrick," she replied pertly. He'd blocked her few remaining game pieces into a corner of the board, and any move she made would result in sweeping defeat.

"Who, then?" he asked mildly.

"Dara Rose, if you must know," Piper said, and then wished she hadn't.

"Ah," he said, as though that explained a great deal. Resigned, she moved her checker piece and he picked up one of his own and leapfrogged over her little band of huddled checkers, one by one. "Let me hazard a guess," he went on, at his leisure, watching her with a smile in his eyes. "You're wondering what to expect when a man and a woman go to bed together, not like we did, but in earnest."

Piper's cheeks flamed, and she knew her eyes were flashing, too. She couldn't bring herself to refute the statement, though she would have liked very much to do just that. "I may be a—a virgin," she sputtered, "but I'm not a complete fool. I *know* what men and women do together."

He began to set up the board for yet another game, concentrating solemnly on the task. "Then why do you want to ask Dara Rose about it?"

"I did not say, at any time, that I wanted to ask my cousin about her very private relationship with her husband," Piper said stiffly. Maybe she *hadn't* said it, but it was very much on her mind, and he'd guessed that, obviously.

"But you do," Sawyer said lightly.

"I do *not,*" Piper lied. This was an unsettling aspect of her new self—skirting the truth—and she didn't approve.

Sawyer's glance strayed toward the front window then, and Piper realized he'd done that a couple of times in the past hour or so. She'd paid it no mind then, figuring he must be thinking about the weather, which was a concern to everybody, but now she sensed that there was another reason. Was he expecting someone? Waiting for something?

He wasn't wearing his gun belt, she noticed now, with relief, but his Colt .45 had somehow found its way to the top of a nearby bookshelf.

"Last game," he said, when the board was ready. He yawned then, but it looked and sounded contrived to Piper.

She studied him suspiciously, decided to call his bluff. "I've had enough of checkers for one night," she told him, rising from her chair and smoothing her skirts, "and this has been a long and trying day." Leaving the nearest lantern for him, she found a second one, struck a match to the wick, wrapped herself in the same old blanket, not wanting to spoil her new cloak, and started for the door.

Sawyer didn't ask where she was going, but he did reach for his .45, shove it under his belt in a disturbingly practiced way, and follow.

"I'm only going to the privy," she whispered, embarrassed.

"Not alone," Sawyer answered. With that, he squired her outside, down the steps, and around to the back of the schoolhouse. The privy loomed ahead, in a faint wash of moonlight.

Much to Piper's relief, he came to a stop at the corner of the school building and stood still, like a guard who took his duty very seriously.

Piper dashed for the outhouse, used it, and hurried out again, holding her breath.

Sawyer remained where he was, looking around, listening.

"What is it?" she demanded, whispering because that seemed to fit the mood of the moment. There was something clandestine about his bearing, and he was so keenly alert she could feel it.

"Nothing," he said, taking her elbow and hustling her around front at such a pace that she nearly stumbled once or twice.

"I don't believe you," Piper said.

He steered her back inside the schoolhouse, shut the door and lowered the latch.

"Go to bed," he told her. "I'll be staying up for a while."

"Why?"

Sawyer turned his gaze to her at last, and she saw a worried smile lurking in his blue eyes. "Would you rather I came with you?" he asked.

She reddened. "Well, no, but—"

"Then go," he broke in, distracted. "I'll put out the lanterns and bank the fire in a little while."

Piper opened her mouth, closed it again. Huffed out a sigh of frustrated curiosity.

"Go," Sawyer repeated.

She went, but only after filling a basin with warm water and carrying it into the bedroom with her.

There, she undressed quickly, gave herself a cursory sponge bath, over in moments, and pulled on her nightgown. She hesitated, debating, then got into the spare bed, where she'd slept the night before.

After a while, the lanterns went out, and she expected Sawyer to join her, but he didn't.

She waited, and then waited some more.

Still no Sawyer. Wasn't he coming to

bed? *His* bed, that is? It was getting late, and he'd extinguished the lanterns, though she hadn't heard the stove door open and then clang shut, so he hadn't banked the fire.

She got up, finally, and crept to the doorway, peering into the gloom of the schoolroom, faintly tinged with moonlight. Once her eyes had adjusted, she could make Sawyer out. He was next to the front window, but not in front of it, as unmoving as the eternal hills.

Piper saw the gun then—he was holding it in his upraised hand, at the ready.

She stifled a gasp.

"Go back to bed, Piper," he said quietly. Until then, she'd thought he hadn't known she was there.

"I want to know what's happening," she insisted.

"Go to bed," Sawyer repeated.

Piper bristled—he had no business giving her orders, being her husband in name only—but she did as he said.

Wriggling down between the covers, she fumed, but she was afraid, too. Something was definitely wrong.

She closed her eyes, not expecting to sleep, and was immediately swallowed up by a shallow, uneasy slumber.

IT WAS JUST a feeling, nothing Sawyer could really put a finger on, but over the years, he'd learned to pay attention to the subtler signs. Ever since supper, the fine hairs on his nape had been raised, and there was a familiar sensation, like the touch of an icy fingertip, dead center in the pit of his stomach.

Hell of a wedding night, he thought wryly. First checkers, and now a vigil alongside a darkened window.

He could see part of the schoolyard from where he stood, being careful not to make a target of himself. The decorated Christmas tree seemed to whisper and sparkle when it captured a stray beam of moonlight, and the desks and stove were nothing but shadows.

Something moved, over by the rope swing dangling from a branch of the oak tree.

A stray dog, probably, or a coyote.

Perspiration tickled his upper lip and his palm felt damp where he gripped the butt of his .45. The wound in his left shoulder throbbed with every heartbeat.

Maybe he was loco—after all, he'd married a woman he'd known for two days, and he'd been delirious part of the time, when he wasn't cotton-headed from the laudanum.

Wasn't that proof that he'd lost his mind?

He swallowed the raspy chuckle that rose to the back of his throat, eased his finger back from the trigger a little. And every instinct urged caution.

There it was again—something moving, more shadow than substance, at least at first. As he watched, holding his breath, silently willing Piper to stay asleep and not come wandering out here to hector him with questions, the shadow took on the shape of a man.

And Sawyer recognized the stance, the way the rifle rested across one forearm with an ease that bespoke long experience.

He'd worked with Chester Duggins, several jobs back, but he hadn't seen him in years, hadn't thought of him, either. If asked, Sawyer would have said Chester was six feet under by now, in some bare-ground-and-thistle cemetery, long forgotten.

"I know you're in there, McKettrick," Duggins called. His voice was quiet, just barely audible, but it carried far enough. "Come on out here, and let's get this over with, so I can collect my money."

Sawyer glanced in the direction of the bedroom, prayed that Piper would stay put. She wouldn't, of course—when she heard the inevitable gunshots, she'd come running. And if Sawyer didn't happen to be the one still standing, Duggins would shoot her, too.

He drew a deep breath, let it out slowly, and moved to the door.

He raised the latch bar, turned the knob as quietly as he could.

Stepped onto the porch, the .45 in his hand, with the hammer drawn back.

"Duggins," he said companionably. "I thought you were dead."

Duggins chuckled in the darkness. He was just a form, with a hat and a rifle, and Sawyer hoped to God that he himself was no more than that to the other man. "Near to it, once or twice," the gunman replied. He hawked and spat. "I thought I'd finished you the other night," he went on, "but darned if I didn't hear otherwise, over at the Bitter

Gulch Saloon. I was laying low over there, waiting out the blizzard, and one of the gals hid me in her room. She told me you were here, living and breathing, getting cozy with the schoolmarm."

Sawyer didn't move. He knew Duggins's friendly chatter was meant to lull him, draw him farther out into the open. Knew there was no way out of this particular confrontation without killing or being killed.

And he was damned if he was going to leave Piper at Duggins's mercy. That, if he recalled correctly, was nonexistent.

"I never figured you for a coward, Chester," Sawyer said easily. They might have been dickering over the price of a horse or a piece of land, from their tone.

Duggins stiffened, raised the rifle slightly. "I was tired of tracking you, McKettrick. Plumb worn to a nubbin. Why, I barely managed to get to this burg before your train came in as it was, and then there was all that snow. Vandenburg had been on me for a good week before that, like stink on a manure pile, wanting you dead." He paused, spat again. "If your death don't turn up in newspapers all over Texas, and right soon, I don't get paid."

Sawyer wasn't surprised to learn that Vandenburg was behind the attack; he'd figured as much. "That," he replied, "would be a real pity."

"Now, don't be thataway!" Duggins whined. "None of this would even be happening if you'd just left the boss man's missus be. Why, if we'd met up in any other circumstances but these, you and me, we'd probably have had a drink together and talked about old times."

"I still think you're a miserable, two-bit coward," Sawyer said cheerfully. He'd heard a sound behind him, in the schoolhouse, and he knew he was almost out of time. Piper was awake, and she'd walk right into this in another few seconds. His tone was easy as he went on. "You bushwhacked me, Chester. In a snowstorm. And you did it that way because you knew you wouldn't have a chance in a fair fight." He stepped down off the porch and moved slowly to one side, so if Duggins fired at him and missed, the bullet wouldn't go right through the schoolhouse door—and Piper's heart.

"I done told you I was fed up with trying to run you to ground," Duggins complained.

"Now, you stand still, and we'll have this out."

"I've already drawn," Sawyer told the other man calmly. "Even if you hit me, which you might not, given how dark it is, I'll still get off at least one shot—more likely, two or three. And you know I'll make them count. So why don't you just lay that rifle down on the ground and step away from it with your hands up, before somebody gets hurt?"

Duggins gave a low, rough bark of laughter, like he was fixing to spit again. "Hell," he said. "You're just trying to talk your way out of this. And you're wasting my time and your breath, because I mean to kill you proper this time."

The whole world seemed to slow down then. Sawyer saw Duggins swing the rifle barrel in his direction, and he'd begun to pull the trigger back on the .45, but before either of them managed to fire, the night ripped apart, rent by a crimson flash of gunpowder and a boom so loud that it rattled the schoolhouse windows.

Duggins folded to the ground, with the gruesome grace of a dancer dying in mid-pirouette. His rifle struck the ground and went off, the bullet making a *whing* sound as it tore away a chunk of the schoolhouse roof.

Sawyer gaped, stunned, his .45 still un-fired in his hand, as Bess Turner stepped out of the darkness and into a thin spill of moonlight, lowering a shotgun, both barrels still smoking, and prodding at Dug-gins's unmoving form with one foot.

"Reckon he's dead?" she asked calmly.

Sawyer approached, crouched to get a better look. She'd blown the back of Dug-gins's head off. "Reckon so," he replied.

"Good," said Bess Turner, with a sigh of resignation.

Meanwhile, Piper flew toward them on a run, her feet bare, her hair loose. "What—?" she began, but her words fell away when she looked down and saw old Chester ly-ing there.

Sawyer wanted to send her back inside, but she wouldn't go and he knew it, so he saved himself the aggravation and stood, wrapping his good arm around her, hold-ing her against his side.

"Varmint," Bess said, and gave the body another poke with her toe, harder this time. The woman's yellow hair was down, and she seemed to be wearing some kind of silky going-to-bed getup, though Sawyer couldn't be sure because the moon had slipped behind a cloud and the stars weren't shining all that brightly.

"Let's go inside," Sawyer said. "Half the town will be here in the next few minutes."

Bess nodded and favored Piper with a thin smile. "You all right, Teacher? This varmint here, he didn't hurt you none?"

"Er—no—I'm—" Piper choked on whatever it was she'd meant to say after that, and fell silent.

Sawyer steered both women toward the gaping door of the schoolhouse. The puny light of a single lantern spilled through it, a kind of faltering welcome, it seemed to him.

Inside, Piper rallied a little, lit several more lamps, and got busy making a pot of tea.

Bess leaned her shotgun against the wall, near the door, and sat down on top of one of the smaller desks, looking as though the events of the past few minutes might be catching up with her at last.

Sawyer took a blanket from Piper's bed, went outside, and draped it over the dead man. It wasn't much—just a gesture, really—but he couldn't leave the damn fool uncovered, staring blindly up at the night sky.

As he'd expected, folks had heard the shots, and some of them were already gathering at the top of the schoolhouse road, a cluster of moving lantern light and muffled noise.

Sawyer sighed and went back inside, where he found Piper still fussing with tea and Bess Turner still sitting on that desk, her gaze fixed on something far away.

"What brought you here tonight?" he asked Bess, very quietly.

Piper paused in her tea-brewing to turn around. Her hair fell around her shoulders, a waterfall of dark curls, and she wore a flannel nightgown. There was mud on her feet, though she didn't seem to care.

"That feller yonder," Bess said, with a toss of her head toward the front of the schoolhouse. "He got one of my girls to hide him, the night of the big snowstorm. She didn't know it was him that shot you—didn't even know it had happened, there at the first—but then, well, these things get around—and Sally Mae, she finally figured out why that galoot was hiding out. She was scared to tell for a while—guess he must have threatened her—but tonight when he got his rifle and lit out on foot, she came and told me. I got my shotgun and followed him, but I was sure wishing Clay McKettrick didn't live way the heck and gone out in the country." Bess paused to draw a shaky breath. "I was here, when that feller called you out, but I wasn't sure what to do. I reckoned if I yelled at him to put the rifle down, he'd probably turn right around and kill me where I stood, so when I saw that he meant to gun you down for sure, I shot him."

Piper's mouth was open. Out of the corner of his eye, Sawyer saw her close it, very slowly.

"You think they'll put me in jail?" Bess fretted, looking over one shoulder as the voices drew nearer. "My Ginny-Sue can't do without a mama—"

"No," Sawyer said. "Nobody's going to put you in jail."

Piper moved to Bess's side, without a word, and slipped an arm around her shoulders.

A vigorous pounding sounded at the door.

Exclamations were raised when somebody evidently stumbled over the blanket-covered body in the schoolyard.

"Hold your horses," Sawyer said, crossing to open the door.

Doc Howard spilled into the room, closely followed by several other men.

"Great scot," Howard nearly shouted, "there's a dead man out there!"

"Yep," Sawyer said.

Attention shifted to Bess, and to Piper, standing stalwartly beside her, chin raised.

Sawyer would forever remember that that was when he realized he was in love with Piper St. James McKettrick, though he supposed it would be a while before he got around to saying so.

"What happened?" Doc demanded.

Sawyer explained, and Piper's eyes seemed to widen with every word he said.

"He's the one that shot you?" Doc said, with a shake of his head. Sawyer had already told them as much, but these were peaceable men, and they had trouble taking it in.

"Well, where the devil are we going to put him?" another man asked. "We don't have an undertaker here in Blue River."

"The jailhouse will have to do, for the time being," Sawyer said.

"Better get him buried first thing tomorrow," Doc put in. "Can't have Christmas spoiled. Do we have to report this to somebody?"

Sawyer nodded. Since he hadn't been sworn in yet, Clay was the logical choice, and he said so. A certificate would have to be drawn up, signed by Judge Reynolds and probably Doc Howard, too.

One of the men agreed to ride out to Clay's place and tell him what had happened.

Sawyer would have preferred to make the visit himself, but he didn't have his horse and, improved though his condition was, he wasn't sure he could make it all that way, anyhow. All this activity had riled up the wound in his shoulder, and it was raising three kinds of hell. Besides, he couldn't leave Piper alone, especially after all that had happened.

When the men went back outside, Sawyer went with them.

Somebody ran to the livery stable, hitched up a buckboard and drove it back to the schoolhouse, and Chester Duggins's mortal remains were hoisted into the back and hauled away.

Doc agreed to make sure Bess Turner got back to the Bitter Gulch Saloon all right, though he seemed nervous about it. Little wonder, Sawyer concluded—that wife of his would kick up some dust if she caught wind of the courtesy.

Inside the schoolhouse, Bess and Piper were sitting there in their nightclothes, calmly sipping tea like two spinsters at a garden club meeting.

The sight touched Sawyer—he thought of how differently this night could have ended. What if Duggins had been startled, and swung that rifle in Piper's direction when she came running out of the school-house door? He might have panicked, pulled the trigger, and killed her.

A headache pounded between Saw-yer's temples, and his stomach did a slow, backward roll.

"Let's get you on home now," Doc said to Bess, blinking at the way she was dressed. Evidently, he hadn't noticed until then.

She set aside her cup, smiled graciously, and stood up. "I'll just fetch my shotgun," she said, turning to Piper. "Thank you very kindly for the tea, Miss St. James. I do appreciate your hospitality."

"You're—you're sure you're not hurt?" Piper asked the other woman.

Bess nodded again, looked briefly at Sawyer. "I'm sure," she told Piper.

Doc had averted his gaze to Piper, but it immediately bounced away again, landing square on Sawyer's face. "I'll stop by in the morning," the dentist said. "Have another look at that shoulder. You in any pain right now?"

"No," Sawyer lied. He wanted to be alone with Piper, that was all, and reflect on the glorious fact that they were both still alive.

Doc looked skeptical, but he escorted Bess and her shotgun out into the night, resigned to walking her home.

Sawyer latched the door behind them, turned, leaning against it, and closed his eyes for a moment, willing himself to stay upright.

"Sawyer?" Piper said, very softly. "You look terrible. I'm going to call Doc Howard back."

But Sawyer shook his head. "I'm just—tired."

She slipped an arm around Sawyer, as if to hold him up, which might have been laughable, given her small stature, if the act itself hadn't eased so many things rioting inside him.

"I'm going to require a lot of answers in the morning," she warned, as they made their slow but steady way across the schoolroom.

Sawyer chuckled at that. "And I'll give them to you," he promised. "In the morning."

SAWYER LANDED HEAVILY on the bed, and barely objected when Piper pulled his boots off his feet and covered him, fully dressed, with the quilts she'd once prized so greatly. She smoothed his hair back from his forehead and bent to kiss his eyelids, first one, and then the other.

He fell asleep so quickly that she worried he'd lost consciousness again, but his breathing was steady and deep, and when she laid her head against his chest, she heard his heart beating with a rhythmic *thud-thud-thud.*

She left him just long enough to put out the lanterns still burning in the schoolroom and bank the fire for the night. He'd set his pistol on one of the desks when he came in earlier, after the shooting, and she picked it up carefully, carried it into the bedroom, and set it on the night table.

For a long time, she sat on the side of the bed, watching him sleep, periodically checking his bandages to make sure he hadn't reopened the wound in his shoulder, but there was no bleeding.

The little room grew colder, and then colder still, and Piper knew she ought to get some sleep herself, but she found she couldn't leave Sawyer, even for the other bed, near as it was.

Finally, shivering, she crawled in beside him, on his right side, snuggling up close for warmth, resting one hand on his strong chest. Again, she felt the thump of his heart against her palm, matched her breathing with his.

And after a while, lulled, she drifted off into sleep, a sound one this time.

The next thing she knew, morning light flooded the room.

Remembering the events of her wedding night, Piper sat bolt upright.

She'd thought Sawyer was still asleep,

but she knew by the slow curve of his lips and the way he eased an arm around her that he was very much awake.

"Good morning, Mrs. McKettrick," he said.

"Who was that man and why did he want to kill you?" Piper replied.

Sawyer chuckled and opened his eyes. His chin was stubbly with gold. "I can't say you didn't warn me you'd have questions," he said, "but I *did* expect we'd both be dressed at the time."

Piper clutched at the quilts, drew them up to her chin in a belated effort at modesty, but did not relent. "Tell me," she said.

Sawyer sighed. "His name was Chester Duggins," he said. "He and I worked together once."

"Why did he want to kill you?" Piper reiterated.

"He was sent by a man named Henry Vandenburg—my former employer." He paused, sighed again, but, to his credit, he held her gaze. "Vandenburg believed—mistakenly, as it happens—that I'd enjoyed a dalliance with his wife."

"Josie," Piper breathed, troubled. She couldn't help recalling the way Sawyer had said the other woman's name, like a plea, in the hours after he was hurt.

"Josie," Sawyer confirmed.

"You cared about her," Piper said.

"I was beginning to," Sawyer replied. "That's why I decided to accept Clay's invitation and come to Blue River."

The admission caused Piper a distinct pang, but she found comfort in one thing: Sawyer was telling her the blunt, unembroidered truth. "Do you still care for Josie?" she asked bravely. "Because, if you do, we can have our marriage annulled. Since we haven't—consummated it yet."

He reached up, stroked the line of her cheek very gently with the back of his right hand. "Is that what you want?" he asked quietly. "An annulment?"

Piper considered that. "I don't know," she said, when a few moments had passed. Then, primly, she added, "Answer my original question, please."

Sawyer grinned, like a choirboy caught being wicked. "I do not hold any tender feelings for Josie," he replied.

"But you were *beginning* to—"

He sighed again. As he lowered his

hand from her cheek, it brushed briefly over her flannel-covered breast, causing the nipple to turn button-hard and bringing a flush to her cheeks. "There have been other women in my life, Piper," he said. "I don't deny that. But you're the only one I've ever married."

She blinked. Was that supposed to be reassuring? *Was* it reassuring?

"How do I know—?" she began.

He laughed. ' *"What if'?"* he teased.

"Are there other jealous husbands out there who want to have you killed?" Piper persisted.

"A few rejected suitors, maybe," Sawyer conceded. "But no husbands, at least as far as I know."

"That isn't funny," Piper objected, flustered.

"If they'd wanted to call me out," he said reasonably, "they would have done it by now."

"What happens next?"

Sawyer's mischievous expression turned more serious. "I get well, and then I deal with Vandenburg," he said.

"Let Clay do that," Piper said quickly,

though she knew even as she spoke that it was a futile request.

"It's not Clay's responsibility," he answered, regretful but earnest. "It's mine."

"No," Piper argued, in the face of certain defeat. "It isn't. This is why there are laws, Sawyer, and men sworn to enforce them—"

"This is my problem," Sawyer said, "and I'll be the one to set it right."

Piper was almost breathless with panic. She'd thought this waking nightmare was over, now that Duggins was dead, but it clearly wasn't. "By doing what?"

"Never mind that," Sawyer told her, drawing her down beside him, holding her close. She resisted at first, but he felt so warm and strong and solid, and she lost herself in that.

They lay together for a long while, both of them engulfed in a kind of sad silence, thinking their own thoughts.

CHAPTER 8

Clay showed up at the schoolhouse soon after the morning fire was built up and the coffee was brewing on the stove, aghast at the news of last night's shooting. Piper and Sawyer were both fully clothed when he finally arrived, she in another inadequate calico, he in trousers and a shirt from his travel trunk.

Having ridden to town on his own gelding, Sawyer's horse, Cherokee, trotting alongside on a lead rope, the erstwhile marshal of Blue River, Texas, left both animals standing in the muddy yard, among ragged patches of dirty snow. A vivid blotch of red remained on the ground where Mr. Duggins had been felled by Bess Turner, making Piper wish for more snow to cover it up.

Sawyer's cousin barely paused to knock, bursting through the front door before Piper could call out a "Come in."

"I'm sorry I couldn't get here before now," Clay announced, passing right on over "good-morning" or even just a "howdy" in his hurry to get Sawyer's report on the events just past. His gaze moved over both of them, probably in search of fresh injury. "It was late when Pete brought word of what happened, and I was tending a sick calf—"

Sawyer, standing near the stove, interrupted with a chuckle. "You might want to hire Bess Turner as marshal, instead of me," he said. "She's mighty good with a shotgun." With that, he poured coffee into a mug and extended it to Clay, who accepted it gratefully.

Piper, wearing an apron to protect her dress, blurted, "Sawyer's got his mind set on going after the man who hired that killer."

"Hold on, now," Clay said, lowering the

coffee to look from one of them to the other in plain consternation. "We're getting ahead of ourselves, here. Tell me what happened, and don't leave anything out."

Sawyer, after slicing a mildly reproving glance at Piper, gave a brief but complete account of all that had happened the previous night.

When he'd heard the whole story, Clay gave a long, low whistle of exclamation, and took a thirsty sip from his coffee mug before saying, *"Damn.* And here it is, almost Christmas."

Piper wasn't sure what the approach of the holiday had to do with anything, but she wasn't clearheaded enough to pursue the matter at the moment.

Sawyer stood calmly, his own coffee in hand, the mug raised almost to his mouth but not quite there. "It was an eventful day," he said. "Piper and I got married."

Clay fairly choked on a mouthful of coffee, but he was grinning when he caught his breath. *"What?"* he said.

"I believe you heard me the first time," Sawyer replied. "Given what my staying here has done to the lady's reputation, there didn't seem to be any other course of action."

Clay peered at Piper, who blushed. "You agreed to this?"

Glumly, twisting her wedding band round and round with the fingers of her right hand, Piper nodded. "Yes," she murmured.

Clay gave a burst of delighted laughter but just as quickly sobered again, his expression turning watchful and wary. "Is this marriage real, or just some kind of ruse to keep the townspeople from gossiping for the rest of the school term?"

There was no need to say that Piper wouldn't be teaching at Blue River again in the fall. For all the good it seemed to be doing her, she *was* married. The school board would probably hire a man to replace her, if they could find one. Failing that, they'd settle for a single woman but, either way, she was as good as out.

"It's real," Sawyer said.

"Sort of," Piper clarified.

"Which is it?" Clay asked, somewhat impatiently, once again looking from one of them to the other. "Real, or 'sort of' real?"

Piper couldn't have answered to save her life. Her throat had closed off and her face felt like it was on fire.

"My wife," Sawyer explained, "is probably referring to the fact that we've yet to consummate the marriage."

Piper's blush deepened. How could the man speak so casually of something so intimately personal? She wanted to throttle him, then and there.

"Oh," said Clay, blushing a little himself. "Well, anyhow, congratulations. Of course Dara Rose will have a thing or two to say about missing out on the wedding, but she'll be pleased, too."

All of them were quiet for a while.

Piper, desperate for something to do, proceeded to walk over and ring the schoolhouse bell, pulling vigorously on the rope, though she knew no one would come to class that day despite the fact that the weather had turned and the trails, if muddy, were passable. There had, after all, been a death, right out there in the front yard, and while the danger was past, folks would probably need a day or two to get used to the idea before they sent their children back.

Clay and Sawyer talked quietly all the

while, though the bell drowned them out, which was fine with Piper.

"You brought Cherokee," Sawyer said to Clay, after the last peal died away. He was standing at the front window then, looking out, and there was no mistaking the relief in his voice. This only underscored Piper's fears—Sawyer would be leaving Blue River, and her, soon.

"I was thinking you might be ready to come out to the ranch with me," Clay admitted to Sawyer, looking a little sheepish when Piper caught his eye. "That was before I knew about the wedding, you understand."

Sawyer smiled. "I'll be staying here until after the Christmas program," he said. "Then, if it's feasible, Piper and I will both head out to your place."

Clay nodded, but he still seemed befuddled. "Shall I take the horse back with me, then?" he asked.

But Sawyer shook his head, turning again to admire the magnificent animal through the grubby glass in the window. "I can't ride much, but I ought to be able to handle a few minutes in the saddle, now and then, just so I don't forget how."

Clay smiled at that, but when he looked Piper's way again, she saw concern in his handsome face. "Well, then," he said, just a little too heartily, "I guess it's a good thing I brought that hay and grain in the other day, on the sledge. One question, though, cousin—how are you going to manage that saddle with only one usable arm?"

"I'll find a way," Sawyer said, without a trace of doubt.

Clay finished his coffee, set his cup down alongside the basin, on the small table near the stove. "You say this Duggins ya-hoo's carcass is laid out over at the jail-house?"

Sawyer nodded. "Doc Howard wants him buried right away," he said dryly. "Figures a funeral might put a damper on Christmas."

Clay nodded, rubbing his chin. Unlike Sawyer, he'd shaved recently, and there was no visible stubble. "That wouldn't do," he murmured thoughtfully. "Wouldn't do at all." He crossed to the door, took his hat from the peg where he'd hung it up coming in. "I'll send a wire to the federal marshal in Austin," he said. "Just a formality, really." He paused, cleared his throat. "Of course I'll be mentioning Henry Vandenburg's part in this."

Piper saw a muscle bunch in Sawyer's jaw, even under his thickening beard. "Nobody can be arrested on mere hearsay, Clay. You know that."

"The federal marshal still has to be told," Clay said. Although his manner was cordial, there was steel in his tone. "What he does with the information is his concern, not ours."

"I want to handle this," Sawyer said, glaring at his cousin.

"Fine," Clay retorted, on his way out. "If there's anything left to *handle* by the time you're fit to travel, you just have at it with my blessing. In the meantime, I'm still marshal and I'll do what needs doing."

Sawyer started to argue, Piper saw, but he ended up giving an exasperated sigh and shoving the splayed fingers of his good hand through his hair in frustration. "All right, then," he said, "but I'm going to the jailhouse with you."

Evidently, Clay was willing to concede that much, if nothing more. "You say Bess Turner shot this fella?" he asked, refraining from helping as his cousin struggled half-way into his coat. Sawyer had a harder time buckling on his gun belt but, some-how, he managed it, and slipped the .45 deftly into the holster.

Chilled, and not by the weather, Piper hurried to the window when the men went outside, watched as Sawyer put a foot in the stirrup of Cherokee's saddle, gripped the horn, and hauled himself up onto the horse's back. She saw him clench his jaw again, once he was in place, and close his eyes briefly, but other than that, he seemed steady.

Clay and Sawyer were gone upward of an hour, during which time Piper hoped in vain for a pupil or two to wander in, hungry for learning. Because she believed with her whole heart and mind that idle hands were the devil's workshop, she polished all the desks, swept the floors, made up the two beds and fussed with the straggly Christmas tree, with its burden of unas-suming decorations.

When the men returned, Doc Howard was with them, on his mule. All three of them looked grimly introspective, and little wonder.

A man was dead.

In the schoolyard, Sawyer dismounted on his own, but he leaned against Cherokee's side for an extra second or so before stepping back and surrendering the reins to Clay, who led the animal around back to the shed.

Doc walked up to the patch of bloody ground and scuffed at it with one foot, as though to kick dirt over the place where death had left its distinctive mark. He conferred with Sawyer for a few moments, then followed Clay to the shed, returning with a rusted shovel in one hand.

While Sawyer watched, his feet planted a little wider apart than usual as if in an effort to maintain his balance, Doc used the shovel to turn up enough ground to hide the blood spot.

Piper stepped back from the window just as Sawyer turned and started for the door. She tried to look surprised when he came inside, closely followed by Doc, but she knew by Sawyer's wry expression that she hadn't fooled him. He'd never glanced in her direction even once, but he'd known she was at the window, watching, just the same.

"I made more coffee," she said, noting the pallor in Sawyer's face.

He merely nodded, and went on into the bedroom. She heard the bedsprings creak as he lay down.

"He might have overdone things a little," Doc remarked quietly, taking off his hat and coat and hanging them both in the cloak-room.

Piper didn't comment on the understate-ment. "Coffee?" she said instead.

Doc nodded. "Please," he said, looking around for a place to sit down. He was a sturdy man, so none of the students' desks would have held him.

Piper pointed to the chair behind her desk, and he took it gratefully. "I'm a den-tist," he said, as though to remind himself and the world at large of his true calling.

She poured his coffee and took it to him, with a slight, sympathetic smile, barely resisting the temptation to pat his shoulder reassuringly and say, "There, there."

Clay came in, having tended to Saw-yer's horse, and looked around for his cousin.

"Sawyer's resting," Piper said. "Coffee?"

"Got any whiskey?" Clay asked.

"Sorry," Piper replied, with a little shake of her head.

Clay sighed and said, "I'll take the coffee, then, please."

While Piper poured the brew, he went into the bedroom, stayed a few moments, and came back with the rocking chair. He offered it to Piper and, when she refused with a shake of her head, sank into it with an exhalation of breath.

Piper gave him the mug. "Did you send that wire?" she asked Clay, keeping her voice down even though she was fairly sure Sawyer wouldn't overhear her anyway. "To the federal marshal in Austin, I mean?"

"Yes," Clay said, after taking a sip of his coffee. "And I told him Duggins claimed he'd been hired by a fellow named Vandenburg."

"Well, then," Piper said, unable to hide her relief, "no doubt someone will investigate." And, thus, she deduced, Sawyer would not go riding off, the moment he was physically able, to confront the man who'd wanted him dead.

Clay pondered that for a while, then said

ruefully, "Sawyer was right. It's mainly hear-say. The marshal might question Vanden-burg, but unless he admits to hiring Duggins, the man's not likely to be arrested."

Piper felt something curl up tight in the bottom of her stomach. How did Dara Rose bear it, being married to a lawman? Was she afraid for Clay every time he pinned on his badge, strapped on a gun belt, and left home to do his job?

"Then *Sawyer* won't be able to get him to admit anything, either," she reasoned, her tone bordering on pettish, though what she really felt was fear.

"Vandenburg hired a killer," Clay re-minded her flatly, "and Sawyer was shot. Something has to be done, Piper."

"Maybe Mr. Duggins committed the crime all on his own," Piper argued, more than a little frantic now. "He was a *crimi-nal.* It could be that Mr. Vandenburg knew nothing about the plan."

"Yes," Clay said dryly, "and St. Nicholas might join us for Christmas Eve supper at the ranch. Men like Duggins don't act on their own, Piper. They take orders from somebody else."

Doc Howard cleared his throat just then,

reminding both Clay and Piper of his presence. It was strange how such a large personage could take up so little thought-space that he went unnoticed.

Piper glowered at Clay and then at Doc, for good measure, and marched into the bedroom to check on Sawyer.

He lay sprawled atop the covers, with his muddy boots on the bed, further staining the already ruined quilt, but Piper's ire ebbed like an outgoing tide at the sight of him.

She approached Sawyer's bedside, smoothed his hair back from his forehead, and smiled a little. The future was full of uncertainty, but, for this moment at least, he was alive and safe, where she could see him, touch him.

She loved Sawyer McKettrick, she realized. What else could this feeling of sweet desolation mean?

Sawyer didn't open his eyes, but he took her hand in his, gave her fingers a brief squeeze, as if he'd read her mind.

Tears brimmed along her lower lashes as she bent and placed the lightest of kisses on his forehead. *I love you*, she told him silently, and then slipped out of the room because Doc had come in again, his sleeves rolled up and his hands still wet from washing, a basin of clean water in his hands and a roll of bandage cloth under one elbow.

Clay was still in the rocking chair when she returned, looking at the Christmas tree, and he stood up quickly when he realized she was there.

"Sit down, Clay," she said quietly.

But Clay shook his head. "I'd best be heading for home, anyway," he said. "There's not much I can do here, and Dara Rose will be watching the road for me."

Piper nodded, thick-throated again. One of these days, she reckoned, she might be "watching the road," too—for Sawyer. Only, unlike Clay, he might never come back to her.

She brought herself up short. She wasn't a real wife to Sawyer, after all, and the schoolhouse wasn't their home. When he was well enough, her "husband" would go his way, and she would go hers.

Clay had read her expression before she realized he was looking at her, guessing her thoughts, and he laid a brotherly hand to one side of her face.

"Give Sawyer a little time," he said. "He'll get things straight in his head pretty soon."

"He's leaving," she said, not meaning to but unable to hold back the certainty that it was so.

"I reckon if Sawyer goes anywhere, he means to take you right along with him," Clay replied, very quietly. "I know you have your doubts, Piper, but Sawyer didn't marry you just to save your reputation. He's a fine man, but he's no martyr, and he could have handled this situation a dozen different ways without standing up with you in front of a preacher."

"Name one," Piper challenged, too proud to cry but wanting to, wanting to very, very much.

Clay chuckled. "Well, he could have sent you to Dara Rose and me, for one thing. There would have been a scandal, sure, but once folks had a chance to jaw about the particulars for a while, they'd have gone on to something else, and you'd be right back here in this schoolhouse, like nothing ever happened. For one thing, teachers aren't that easy to come by, way out here. The pay's pitiful, and it's a hard, lonely life."

Piper gave a small, strangled laugh. "How comforting," she said. "What was I worried about, when I have a 'pitiful' stipend and a hard, lonely life to look forward to?"

Clay grinned, shook his head. "I've never been good with words," he allowed. "What I'm trying to say is that everything will be all right in the end."

"I can't imagine what makes you so sure of that," Piper observed.

"Just the same," Clay countered good-naturedly, "I *am* sure. Besides, it's almost Christmas. Have a little faith, will you?"

Have a little faith, will you?

Clay's offhand injunction played in Piper's mind long after Doc and Clay had both left the schoolhouse.

Easy enough for him to say, she concluded, as she built up the fire and rummaged through the food box in the cloakroom for the makings of a simple meal.

Upon awakening, Sawyer still looked like hell-warmed-over, but he insisted on joining her in the schoolroom for supper. She gave him the desk chair again, and refrained from conversation since he looked a mite grumpy. His fresh bandages were bulky under his sling, and perhaps a little too tight.

"Clay's gone home?" he asked, finally.

Piper refrained from pointing out the obvious. "Yes," she said mildly. "He fed and watered Cherokee before he left, and brushed him down, too."

Sawyer nodded, thanked her when she put a plate in front of him, containing scrambled eggs, some fried ham, and two thick slices of bread toasted on top of the stove. Ate slowly and awkwardly, and with a dignity that pinched Piper's heart.

"In a few days, it will be Christmas," she said, finding the silence unbearable.

"Yes," Sawyer said dully. She knew without asking what was bothering him, or part of it, at least. The aftermath of a death was always sobering, and on top of that, he'd found riding a horse, something he'd probably done almost every day of his life, with unthinking ease, to be suddenly difficult.

"I wonder how Bess is holding up," Piper said. She'd nibbled on some toasted bread earlier, while cooking, but she really wasn't very hungry, so she hadn't filled a plate for herself.

"To hear Doc tell it," Sawyer answered, his eyes bleak, "she's got other concerns. Her little girl's come down with something."

"Ginny-Sue is sick?" Piper asked, immediately concerned.

Sawyer nodded. "Doc wanted to go and see her, but his wife put her foot down. Said she'd leave him, and take their daughter with her, if he showed his face in a brothel, no matter what the reason."

Piper thought of Ginny-Sue's beaming delight over memorizing the second chapter of Luke, her parting assurance that Christmas would happen for certain now, with the big snowstorm over.

And she put one trembling hand to her mouth.

Sawyer, seeing her face, looked regretful. "Doc said it was probably nothing serious," he said. "Sure, Bess is worried, but you know how mothers are."

Piper was already on her feet, hurrying into the cloakroom, taking the lovely russet cape from its hook and swinging it around her shoulders. She was raising the hood to keep the wind from stinging her ears as she emerged into the schoolroom.

Sawyer was standing by then. "Hold on a second," he said, frowning. "Where are you going? It's dark out, Piper, and it's cold."

"Drat that Eloise Howard," Piper muttered, and that had to suffice for an answer. "I'll be back as soon as I can."

With that, she left the schoolhouse.

It *was* dark, and the wind was brisk, but her cape protected her.

As she crossed the yard, Sawyer called to her from the doorway of the school. "Piper, wait! I'll come with you—"

She turned, still walking, but backward. "You'll be nothing but a hindrance," she called in response. "Stay here, please."

"Piper!" Sawyer yelled, when she turned her back on him again and marched onward.

Thinking only of Ginny-Sue, Piper picked up her pace.

Passing the churchyard, she saw the new grave, where Mr. Duggins had been laid to rest, God forgive him. She wondered if he'd had family somewhere, parents or a wife and children, say, and if anybody would shed tears of sorrow when word of his passing reached them.

On the main street of town, the businesses and shops were all closed up and dark. Except, of course, for the Bitter Gulch Saloon, which seemed to be doing a rousing trade, as usual.

Piper stopped on the plank sidewalk, eyeing the swinging doors with trepidation. Light spilled over and under them, like some smoky liquid, and the tinny clinkity-clink of an out-of-tune piano, badly played, tinkled in the cold air.

Deciding, after much personal deliberation, that she wasn't quite bold enough to walk through those rickety doors into the sawdust heart of a saloon, Piper bustled around back, moving between the buildings, and approached the much less daunting rear entrance.

Standing on a small porch with her chin high and her shoulders squared, she knocked purposefully.

A rotund black woman answered, wide-eyed at the sight of Piper. She laid one hand to her substantial bosom and sucked in a shocked breath. "Lord, have mercy," she said. "It's the schoolmarm!"

Piper drew a deep breath. "Let me in, please," she said. She'd seen the woman once or twice, over at the mercantile, but they'd never exchanged more than a few words. "I've come to look in on Ginny-Sue."

"But, ma'am," the woman argued, "this here's a *bawdy* house!"

As if she hadn't known. Piper looked over one shoulder, half expecting to see Sawyer in pursuit, but he hadn't caught up to her yet. She met the cook's horrified gaze again and whispered, "Hurry. There's no time to lose."

The woman stepped back, admitting Piper to a large and amazingly ordinary kitchen, well-equipped, with a big cast-iron cookstove, bins for sugar and flour, a table surrounded by matching chairs, and a cabinet filled with lovely china. There was even a sink.

"You really shouldn't be here," insisted Bess Turner's cook, in an anxious whisper. "Anybody sees you, there'll be hell to pay!"

Piper put out a hand and introduced herself as Mrs. McKettrick, rather than Miss St. James. It was a small indulgence, she thought. No harm in pretending for a little while.

"Cleopatra Brown," the cook responded.

Her eyes looked enormous in her round ebony face. "You wait here, and I'll fetch Miss Bess."

Piper had spotted the rear stairway by then, and she wanted to climb it, open doors until she found Ginny-Sue, see the child for herself. If Ginny-Sue was seriously ill, she meant to get Doc Howard by the collar and *drag* him over here, and to the devil with any objections *Mrs.* Howard might raise.

She paced while Cleopatra was out of the room, went once or twice to peek through the misted-over window in the back door, in case Sawyer had tracked her this far.

Of course, he, being a man, would probably enter by the *front* way.

The rush of annoyance at the idea sustained Piper in the face of her already waning courage.

After a few minutes—very *long* minutes—Bess descended the rear stairway, be-feathered and be-jeweled, with her face painted like a garish mask. Cleopatra hovered close behind.

"You shouldn't have come," Bess fretted, pausing halfway down, but there was a spark of something that might have been hope in her jaded eyes.

"Nevertheless, I have," Piper replied briskly. "I must know about Ginny-Sue. How is she?"

"She's poorly," Bess admitted, coming the rest of the way down the stairs. "She's real poorly. It came on sudden-like—she was playing outside without her hat and mittens—said she'd found a cat hiding in the woodpile and she was trying to get it to come inside for some warm milk—"

Piper took both Bess's hands, found them colder than her own, even after the walk from the schoolhouse. "I'll get Doc Howard," she said.

"He won't come," Bess said, with sad certainty.

"He *will*," Piper replied, "if I have to drag him!"

Bess smiled tentatively. "If you'd just say howdy to Ginny-Sue, I'm sure that would bring her right around," she said. "She thinks you hung the moon right up there in the sky, you know."

Piper's eyes burned. "Take me to her," she said. "Please."

Bess nodded once, turned, and led the

way back up the staircase to the second floor, her thin shoulders stooped and mostly bared by the scantiness of her dress. Cleopatra moved aside to let both women pass, but she didn't look at all congenial, no doubt thinking that nothing good could come of the schoolmarm's highly improper visit to the upper reaches of a brothel.

Piper might have conceded the point, if challenged, but she didn't hesitate, let alone turn back.

The upstairs hallway was lined with gilt-framed mirrors, and there was a costly runner, probably Turkish, on the floor. The air smelled of talcum powder, stale sweat, and quiet depravity.

To know that little Ginny-Sue was growing up in this place was almost more than Piper could endure. Given her druthers, she'd have bundled the child up in a blanket and physically carried her out of here, never to return.

Bess stopped in front of a door and rapped lightly at the framework. "Let me in, Emmie," she called out softly.

Piper heard a key turn in the lock, and the door creaked open, revealing a scrawny, bare-faced woman clad in a red silk wrapper. Emmie, presumably.

Relieved to learn that someone had been sitting with Ginny-Sue, and that there was a locked door to protect her from unwanted visitors, Piper smiled at Emmie, though only slightly.

Emmie, stepping back to admit them, widened her eyes. Piper concluded that she probably looked as exotic to the other woman as Emmie did to her.

"She's no better," Emmie said to Bess.

The inside of that room was a revelation to Piper, at complete odds with the structure that surrounded and upheld it, but at the moment she was concerned only with Ginny-Sue.

The little girl lay in a huge and elegant bed, with gilt posts and a painting of sheep and shepherdesses on the headboard. She opened her eyes, smiled a tiny smile when she saw Piper.

"I know the whole second chapter of Luke," Ginny-Sue said.

"Shhh," Piper said, smoothing back the child's hair. Her forehead was hot and dry, though the front of her finely embroidered nightgown clung damply to her small chest. "How do you feel?"

"My throat hurts," Ginny-Sue confided, and her hand fluttered up to rest there, fragile as a hatchling bird.

Piper blinked back tears. Smiled. "Maybe you've been practicing your piece too much—for the Christmas program, I mean."

Ginny-Sue smiled back, but the effort seemed to exhaust her. "Is it Christmas yet?" she asked. "Did I miss the program?"

Piper shook her head quickly. "No, sweetheart. Christmas is still a few days away."

Emmie and Bess slipped out, leaving teacher and pupil alone.

Ginny-Sue closed her eyes, but the smile lingered, faint, on her lips.

Piper looked around then, noticed the fireplace, with a lovely blaze burning on the hearth, the velvet draperies on the windows, the carpets on the floor. Paintings of flowers, delicately wrought in watercolor, graced the walls. There were easy chairs, upholstered in cheery prints, and a door opened onto a bathroom. She could see the side of a long porcelain tub. And there was electricity, at least here, if nowhere else in the Bitter Gulch Saloon.

This, then, was the haven Bess Turner had made for her child, a place apart, a world that belonged only to the two of them.

Piper turned back to Ginny-Sue, gently took her hand, and seated herself on the edge of the fancy bed.

Then she closed her eyes and she prayed.

Ginny-Sue slept on.

Cleopatra came back into the room, bringing a tray laden with tea things. "There's a man downstairs," she said solemnly. "Says you'd better come and talk to him." China rattled as she set the tray down, poured fragrant, steaming orange pekoe into a translucent cup. "What do you want me to tell him?"

"Does he have one arm in a sling?" Piper asked calmly.

"Yes, ma'am, he do," Cleopatra answered.

Sawyer, of course. "Tell him to fetch Doc, or send somebody else if he's not strong enough. Whoever goes is to say that if

Mrs. Howard objects, I'll come over there myself and see to the matter personally, and she does not want that to happen."

Cleopatra's eyes widened again, and a smile rested lightly on her full mouth. "Sounds like a bluff to me," she said, but there was respect in her tone.

"Sometimes," Piper answered, "a bluff has to do."

CHAPTER 9

Half an hour passed, during which Piper sipped tea, listened to the tick of the elegant clock on the mantelpiece, and watched Ginny-Sue toss and turn in her sleep.

Don't let this be diphtheria, Piper prayed, over and over again. *Please.*

She'd seen that disease too many times, in the few years she'd been teaching school. Among the symptoms were fever and a sore throat, and Ginny-Sue had both. Diphtheria was rampantly contagious, and in most instances it was fatal, as well.

Not Ginny-Sue, she pleaded silently, *or any of the others.*

When a tentative knock sounded at the door of that incongruously grand bedchamber, Piper leaped up, crossed the floor, but then hesitated to turn the shining brass key protruding from the lock, remembering that there was a saloon directly downstairs, and that ladies of the evening and their customers surely frequented the other rooms along the corridor.

"Who's there?" she asked.

"Doc and me," Sawyer answered. "Open up."

Almost breathless with relief, Piper unlocked and opened the door to see a disgruntled Doc Howard standing nervously in the hall, with Sawyer right beside him. Doc looked as though he might bolt at any moment, while *Sawyer* looked as though he'd stop him if he did.

"You came," Piper cried, barely restraining herself from throwing both arms around Doc and hugging him in a fit of gratitude.

"Of course I did," Doc replied, stepping past her and striding over to the bed. He'd brought his bag and hopefully there was something inside that would cure Ginny-Sue. "Why is it that nobody around here seems to remember that I'm a dentist?" he muttered to himself, as he leaned over the child, stethoscope in place.

Did dentists use stethoscopes? she wondered. Evidently so. Perhaps some of their patients suffered palpitations at the prospect of an extraction, or having a cavity filled.

Sawyer smiled at Piper, touched her chin. His fingers were icy-cold, and yet, somehow, he warmed her. Had he walked to Doc's place, in his condition, after following Piper to the saloon earlier? If so, he was probably coming to the end of his strength, considerable as it was.

"I'm all right," he told her quietly. It was unsettling, the way he seemed to be able to read her every expression, as if she'd been thinking aloud. "How's the little girl?"

"I don't know," Piper responded, worried again. "She's feverish, and she told me her throat was hurting."

"Doc will do everything he can," Sawyer promised. He indicated his bandaged shoulder with a motion of his head and then added, "He must be hell on a toothache, if he's this good with a bullet wound."

Piper nodded anxiously but offered no reply, since none seemed called-for.

Bess appeared, letting herself in, since Piper hadn't bothered to relock the door. With Sawyer and Doc both there, she knew Ginny-Sue would be safe.

After nodding a greeting to Sawyer, Bess hurried over to stand on the opposite side of the bed from Doc. She wrung her hands, and the expression in her eyes was an eloquent plea for good news.

Doc opened his bag, took out a packet, and held it up. "Headache powders," he said. "Stir a teaspoonful into a cup of water, and we'll see if we can't get her to take it."

Bess rounded the bed, took the packet from Doc's hand, and vanished into the bathroom. She was back in a trice with the water, and Piper handed her a spoon from the tea tray Cleopatra had brought up earlier.

The rattle of the spoon against the glass roused Ginny-Sue enough to open her eyes. They glistened, too bright, and seemed to grope and struggle from one face to the next.

"Mama?" Ginny-Sue said.

"I'm right here, baby," Bess said, moving close to the child, sliding an arm around her to help her sit up, forcing cheer into every word and motion, "you've got to drink this whole glass of water right down. Doc brought you some medicine, and it's going to make you feel a lot better, real soon."

Ginny-Sue's confusion was heartrending for Piper, and she was thankful when Sawyer put his good arm around her waist, lending her strength. Almost holding her up, in fact.

The child sipped from the glass, the bitter taste causing her to wince, and it obviously hurt her to swallow. Still, though the process was a long one, she finally emptied the glass.

"What is it?" Piper whispered to Doc, when he walked over to her and Sawyer, looking solemn and thoughtful, though he'd left his bag on the night table and was taking off his coat like a man who meant to stay rather than go. "What's wrong with Ginny-Sue?"

"If we're lucky, she's got a bad cold," Doc answered, keeping his voice low. "If we're not, on the other hand, then this is probably diphtheria, and it works fast. We ought to know by morning."

Piper reached out, took one of Doc's

hands in both of hers. Sawyer stood silently beside her.

"Thank you," she said softly, because she knew Doc had made a sacrifice to come here at all.

Doc's smile was genuine, if somewhat feeble. "Don't thank me yet," he replied. "The aspirin powders will bring down the girl's fever if she's just taken a chill, but if that doesn't happen, well, then we're dealing with a much bigger problem."

"Diphtheria," Piper almost whispered.

Doc nodded. "None of us can leave here until we know for sure," he said, with a rueful shake of his head. "If this *is* diphtheria, it'll spread like a fire in dry grass."

Piper looked at Sawyer, whose expression was unreadable, and then Doc. By then, Bess had left Ginny-Sue's side to join them.

"Did you say my girl has diphtheria?" Bess asked tentatively, going pale under all that kohl and rouge and rice powder.

"I said she *might* have it," Doc said, at once stern and compassionate. "How long has Ginny-Sue been sick?" Before Bess could formulate a reply—she seemed to be juggling conflicting thoughts in her mind—he turned to Piper. "Did she come down with this at school?"

"Just since this afternoon," Bess said finally. "Cleopatra said she seemed fine at breakfast."

"And at school, too," Piper added, after reviewing her memory. Even though Ginny-Sue hadn't exhibited symptoms in class, when all the children had been busy decorating the Christmas tree, it was still possible that the illness was already spreading from one end of Blue River to the other. Edrina—Harriet—little Jeb, the new baby—

She wouldn't be able to bear losing a one of them, or any of her pupils, either.

She almost swooned at the enormity of the threat, but Sawyer took a firm grip on her elbow and steadied her, kept her upright.

He guided her to one of the easy chairs near the fireplace and sat her down.

"What about my girls, and the customers?" Bess asked Doc. "Shouldn't they be told?"

"If you say the word *diphtheria,*" Doc replied, "there'll be a panic for sure. On the other hand, we can't have those men carrying the sickness home to their own families. I'll put the whole place under quarantine before I let that happen." He paused, grim and brusque. "I just hope it isn't already too late."

From her chair near the fire, Piper watched tears gather in Bess's eyes. "We'll see that the beer and whiskey flow," she said quietly. "And those that don't pass out, well, maybe the girls can keep them here some other way."

Some other way, Piper thought, half-sick. Innocent or not, she knew what that "other way" was, and the ugliness of it nearly overwhelmed her.

But who was she to judge? In Bess's shoes, with Bess's history and lack of choices, she'd probably be no different.

Doc gave a heavy sigh, nodded in agreement with what Bess had said. He had a child to worry about, too, Piper reminded herself, his Madeline. Doc Howard's daughter was probably a large part of the reason he'd finally braved his wife's disapproval, after refusing once, and answered Piper's summons.

Unless, of course, Sawyer had forced

the other man to the Bitter Gulch Saloon, at gunpoint. She didn't think he'd be above that.

The possibility made Piper sit up very straight, stiff-spined. "Did you—persuade Doc to come?" she asked, fixing her tired eyes on Sawyer.

"Now, how would I do that, with just one good arm?" he countered.

Piper raised both eyebrows, thinking of the Colt .45 her husband was wearing on his right hip, even then. "One way comes immediately to mind," she said.

Sawyer grinned. "Fortunately," he said, picking up on her meaning right away, "I didn't have to threaten anybody. I guess Doc just figured if I thought it was important enough to ride bareback to his place with a big hole in my shoulder, he ought to pay attention."

Piper scooted her chair a little closer to Sawyer's, dropped her voice to barely more than a breath while Doc and Bess conferred over by the door. "Didn't *Mrs.* Howard have something to say about it?"

Sawyer's grin broadened. "Oh, she had *plenty* to say. Told Doc she'd get on the train and head East if he set foot outside the house, never mind heading straight for a brothel, where God only knew what he might bring home. Yes, sir, she'd leave him high and dry. He said she oughtn't to make promises she didn't mean to keep, got his bag, and followed me over here. Didn't even take the time to saddle his mule."

Piper was wide-eyed. "You heard all that?"

Sawyer nodded. "I was downright proud of the man," he added.

"If I wasn't so grateful," Piper replied, "I'd have a few things to say *myself,* Mr. McKettrick, about you riding around on a horse in the dark of night in your condition."

"It seemed like a better idea than walking," Sawyer pointed out. "I couldn't saddle Cherokee—it's practically impossible to tighten a cinch with one arm—but he didn't complain. I put a bridle on him, led him out of the shed and over to the porch, and climbed on from there."

"I don't suppose it ever occurred to you to heed me and stay put at the schoolhouse?" Piper retorted, though she wasn't actually angry, just fearful to think of all the things that could have gone wrong. Might *still* go wrong.

"I'll always hear you out," Sawyer said, quietly reasonable. "You're an intelligent woman and most of the time your opinion will probably make sense. That said, if I'm not swayed by your arguments, I'll go right ahead and do whatever strikes me as the best choice."

Piper had no reply for that. She was almost too tired to think.

Doc disappeared into the bathroom then and closed the door, while Bess stretched out on the bed alongside her feverish daughter, holding the little girl close, murmuring a lullaby to her.

Though she was still worried sick about Ginny-Sue and every other child in and around Blue River, Piper went over the things Sawyer had said, oddly exhilarated by them, even in her weariness. Yes, he was letting her know that, as a husband, he wouldn't bend to the kind of pressure women like Eloise Howard exerted, but it was the word *always* that had really caught her attention. He'd sounded as if he expected to share his life with her—as if they'd be working out problems and disagreements *years* from now.

"I thought you were leaving," she said carefully. "Heading out to find Mr. Vandenburg as soon as you could ride that far."

"I might still do that," Sawyer answered, one corner of his mouth quirking upward ever so slightly. "But I've done some thinking since last night, about how close I came to losing you when it was me Duggins was after. When you bolted from the schoolhouse a little while ago, hell-bent on storming the Bitter Gulch Saloon for the sake of a sick child, and devil take the gossip that was bound to result, I knew you were the one for me."

Piper sat stunned, stricken by hope even in this uncertain and potentially tragic situation. How was it possible for one person to contain so many powerful emotions, especially ones that were at odds with each other?

Doc emerged from the bathroom, drying his hands on a towel and glancing toward Ginny-Sue, and the woman who was holding her.

"That's quite a setup in there," he commented, cocking a thumb over one shoulder to indicate the bathroom. "Running water, hot and cold. Even a flush toilet." Doc paused then to rub his chin and reflect for a moment or two. "If I put in a bathtub over at our place, I reckon Eloise might decide I'm a passable husband, after all."

Sawyer grinned as Doc pulled over an ottoman and sat down close to the fire, rubbing his hands together and staring into the flames.

"And if she doesn't change her mind?" Sawyer asked.

Piper nudged his foot with her own, but he was undaunted and, anyway, it was already too late to stop him from asking such a personal question.

Doc chuckled, the firelight dancing over his face. "Well, then," he answered, "I may be forced to take a pretty fierce stand."

After that, all three of them alternately dozed and talked in quiet voices.

The fire got low, and Doc built it up again.

Once, feeling restless, Piper ventured into the bathroom and inspected the gleaming porcelain bathtub, trying all the while to imagine the sheer luxury of such a convenience. No water to pump or haul up from the well in a bucket, then heat on the stove, then carry and pour, and repeat the whole process all over again. Why, it would be miraculous—even better, at least in her opinion, than a private telephone and electric lights put together.

Around sunrise, pinkish-gold light glowing cold and clear at the windows, Cleopatra returned with another tray, knocking politely at the bedroom door and calling out in a low voice, "Somebody open this door for me. I've got my hands full out here."

This time, she'd brought fresh coffee, along with cups to drink it from, and a heaping plate of cinnamon buns still warm from the oven. The aromas were heavenly.

Concentrating hard, Cleopatra nearly dropped the whole works when a small voice suddenly piped up and said, "Mama? Did I miss Christmas?"

Everyone turned toward the bed to see Ginny-Sue sitting up, pillows at her back, looking a little wan but clear-eyed and alert.

Bess, who had slept beside Ginny-Sue through the night, gathered the child close again and wept for joy. "No, baby," she said, beaming through her tears. "You didn't miss Christmas. You surely didn't!"

Doc went over to touch Ginny-Sue's forehead, and his broad smile told the story. The fever had broken.

"That's one of the finest chest colds I've ever seen," Doc said, in a jocular voice that nonetheless cracked with fatigue. "A few days of bed rest and I'll wager the little lady here is good as new."

Piper turned immediately into Sawyer's embrace, trembling a little, weak with relief. She felt his lips move against her temple. "Go ahead and cry," he told her softly, patting her back. "God knows, you've earned the right."

THERE WOULD BE no school that day, fortunately for Piper, who probably couldn't have kept her eyes open to teach. Doc gave a dime to the local newspaper boy and told him to spread the word, along with the just-printed edition of the weekly *Blue River Gazette.*

He and Sawyer shook hands, and Piper greeted Cherokee, who'd stood patiently at the hitching rail all night long, even though he'd come untied at some point. Stroking the horse's velvety nose, she promised him an extra ration of grain.

Then Doc headed off toward his place, doubtless girding his loins for battle as he went, and Piper and Sawyer made for the schoolhouse, in the other direction, Sawyer leading Cherokee along behind.

Piper couldn't recall when she'd ever been so tuckered out, or so full of happiness. There would be no outbreak of diphtheria, at least for the time being, and Ginny-Sue was going to be all right.

As soon as they'd reached the schoolhouse, Sawyer put Cherokee away in the shed, and Piper went along, partly to help, and partly to keep her word about the grain.

While Sawyer removed Cherokee's bridle and then proceeded to give the animal a quick brushing down, Piper plunged a hand into one of the feed sacks Clay had brought in from the ranch and held out her palm, heaping with grain.

"Watch your fingers," Sawyer warned, but he was smiling as he spoke.

Piper just laughed.

Cherokee ate delicately, for a big-jawed

creature with enormous teeth, and Piper patted his head when he'd finished, and called him a good boy.

"Hey," Sawyer teased. "I'm starting to get jealous."

Piper made a face at him, but then she sobered a little. "Do you think Doc will really stand up to Eloise?" she asked.

Now it was Sawyer who laughed. Having been on the other side of the horse, he ducked under Cherokee's long neck and came up in front of Piper like a swimmer breaking the surface of still waters.

"No," he said. His voice was sleepy and low, and he still needed a shave. "I think he'll bribe her with a fancy bathtub and an indoor toilet, and she'll let him off the hook—until next time, anyway."

She felt incredibly shy, all of a sudden. Maybe it was from lack of sleep. "The poor man *is* a dentist," she said.

Sawyer laughed again. "Come on, Mrs. McKettrick," he said. "Let's get you inside so you can get some shut-eye."

They went into the schoolhouse, and Sawyer headed for the stove to build a fire while Piper hung up her beautiful russet-colored cloak. She'd never owned a finer garment in all her life, but she was too worn out just now to properly appreciate it.

She wandered into the bedroom, taking off everything but her bloomers and camisole in the shadowy cold, and practically dove into bed, anxious to get warm.

It was only when she caught a fleeting glimpse of Sawyer standing in the doorway that she realized she'd gotten into the wrong bed, the one she was in the habit of sleeping in.

And she was not about to risk more goose bumps by getting out again.

There was a fire going in the stove, she could smell the burning wood and hear the popping, but the warmth was still far away.

"A man could misinterpret aspects of this situation," Sawyer remarked, crossing to sit down on the edge of the bed, right next to her.

She realized then that she must have dozed off for a while, because he was clean-shaven, and his skin and hair, which was damp, smelled of soap.

Piper yawned, stretched luxuriously.

"Really?" she asked coyly. For some incomprehensible reason, she'd forgotten how to be afraid, how to mistrust another person's motives. If that other person happened to be Sawyer McKettrick, that is.

"Oh, yes," Sawyer replied seriously, kicking off his boots. "That could easily happen."

"What if a *woman* wanted to be held, for example?" Piper's voice was a little shaky now, and her heart was picking up speed with every beat. She'd only had this feeling once before, when she was much younger and speeding down a snowy hillside in Maine on a homemade toboggan.

"That could be arranged," Sawyer said, after pretending to give the prospect due consideration. "But he might be tempted to, well, *persuade* her a little—beyond holding her, that is."

"I guess that would be acceptable," Piper allowed, from beneath the covers.

Sawyer chuckled, and there was some shifting around, and then he was in the bed beside her—her *husband*—resting one hand on the curve of her hip. "It might take days," he said, his voice husky, "but I'm a patient man."

"You are not," Piper argued, as he uncovered her face and quieted her with a kiss.

It was light and soft at first, that kiss, but it soon gathered momentum.

As Sawyer kissed her, he undid the laces at the front of her camisole. "Oh, but I am," he disagreed, when their mouths parted. "Patient, I mean."

Piper slipped her arms around his neck, gasped when he opened the camisole and bared her breasts. Stroking one, chafing the nipple gently with the side of his thumb, he nibbled his way down over her collarbone.

"How could it—take—days?" she asked, a little out of step with the flow of conversation.

"I like to take my time," Sawyer replied, measuring out the words slowly, so slowly, like a man muttering in his sleep. "Especially when I'm doing this." And then his mouth closed, warm and wet and pulling ever so gently, around her already distended nipple.

She cried out with pleasure, instinctively arched her back in a plea for more and then still more.

"Days," Sawyer said idly, moving to her other breast.

The pleasure—yes, it *was* pleasure, and it was glorious, and it was *hers*—unleashed something inside Piper, some vast, elemental state of derring-do she hadn't known existed.

Over the next few minutes—or was it hours?—Sawyer raised Piper to a fever pitch with his fingers, his lips, his words. She wriggled out of her bloomers with a shameful lack of encouragement, making him laugh.

When he slid his hand between her legs and began to work her with a light, circular motion of the heel of his palm, she was lost. And then he took her nipple into his mouth again, and she was electrified, more completely and powerfully *alive* than ever before.

"Oh—*Sawyer*—" she sobbed out.

He lifted his head from her breast, where he'd been feasting, and said quietly, "Any time you want me to stop, Piper, all you have to do is say the word and I will."

"Ooooooh," she moaned, raising her hips high off the mattress to maintain contact with his hand. *Stop?* Not if she had anything to say about it.

He quickened the pace of his hand, and she went wild with desire, with a need that would not be refused. "There's more," he told her softly, gruffly, tracing the length of her neck with his lips. "There's a lot more. But before any of that happens, I want you to know how it's supposed to feel when I make love to you."

She cried out again, frenzied, flying. Wanting. She was wanton, wide open to him, and she felt no shame, only freedom and ferocious instincts.

"Sawyer!" she pleaded raggedly.

"Let go," he murmured. "Just let go."

There was a fierce seizing sensation then, deep inside her, a thing of the spirit as well as the body, followed by a release so keen that it seemed to consume all of Piper in sweet blazes of satisfaction. Her body flexed and flexed again, speaking its own language of joy.

Finally, she shattered completely and, after what seemed like a very long time, fell back into herself, in a slow but still dizzying drop, dazed, crooning and purring with every small aftershock.

"That's how it's supposed to feel," Sawyer told her, with a grin, much later, when her breathing had returned to something approaching normality and her heart had ceased struggling to flail its way out of her chest and fly heavenward like a bird.

She snuggled against Sawyer. "But there's more," she repeated sleepily.

"Yes," Sawyer said, with a smile in his voice. His chin was propped on the top of her head. "We'll have time for that later."

"Mmmmm," she said, and moved closer still.

Then she felt the hard length of him against her thigh, and she was instantly wide awake.

"I did say there was more," Sawyer reminded her, his eyes alight with mischief and—just possibly, no it couldn't be, not so soon—love.

"Now I know why everyone says it hurts," Piper announced, feeling her eyes go wide.

"Everyone?" Sawyer asked, teasing. "Is this something you talk about a lot?"

She shook her head, nervous and, at the same time, wanting him. All of him. "Of course not," she whispered, as though imparting a secret in the midst of a listening crowd. "But, well, it does seem—logistically impossible."

At that, Sawyer threw back his head and gave a shout of laughter.

She thumped his chest with the side of one fist, though not very hard. "What's so funny, Sawyer McKettrick?" she demanded, blushing from her hairline to her toes.

He didn't answer right away, but his amusement subsided a little.

Their gazes locked and the mood turned serious again.

"*Will* it hurt?" she asked meekly.

"Probably," Sawyer answered, smoothing her hair away from her cheek. "But only the first time, and for just a little while."

"Oh," Piper said.

"It's up to you," he reiterated.

"Let's try," Piper decided.

"It's not like that," Sawyer told her. "There's no 'try.' You do it, or you don't do it."

"Will it hurt you?"

He kissed her forehead, then the tip of her nose. "No," he answered, in his forthright way.

"And there's only pain the first time?"

He nodded. "Usually. And I'll be real careful, I promise."

She believed him. Her heart widened somehow, and took him in, and that was the moment she truly became his wife. "I love you, Sawyer," she said, and she'd never meant anything more than she meant those words. "I know you probably don't—"

He stopped her from finishing the sentence by pressing an index finger to her lips. "I can speak for myself, woman," he said, with mock sternness. "And it just so happens that I love you, too. I realized it when you took off for the Bitter Gulch Saloon—even before that, really—to see to Ginny-Sue, and there was no talking you out of it."

She blinked. "Really? Why?"

He gave another raspy chuckle and shook his head. "I guess I admire spirit in a woman," he replied, "and you've got plenty of that, all right, with some to spare."

His answer pleased her deeply, settled into her, saturated her with a sense of rightness and perfect safety. "Well, Mr. McKettrick, I think it's about time we consummated our marriage, don't you?"

"You're sure?" He looked troubled, but blue-green fire burned in his eyes.

"I'm absolutely positive," she replied.

Dutifully, she situated herself on the mattress, spread her legs a little, and waited for him to get on top of her.

Instead, he gave another chuckle, and then he drove her to near madness again, caressing her, kissing her, whispering things that made her blood rush hot through her veins.

When Sawyer finally took Piper for his own, in a long, swift thrust, she wanted, *needed* him inside her so much that she barely noticed the twinge of pain as her maidenhead gave way.

Her body responded to his, as if drawing on some ancient knowledge, stroke for stroke, giving and then taking, offering and then demanding, and when he finally stiffened upon her, with a hoarse cry, and she felt him spilling himself into her, ecstasy claimed her once again, even more completely than before, and her cry of triumph rose to meet and mingle with his.

Later, they slept, and it seemed to Piper, as she drifted off, exhausted and utterly spent, a vessel deliciously emptied of all she had to give, that even though their bodies were separate and distinctly individual, their souls had somehow fused into one being, a making-right of many wrongs, large and small, a kind of coming home to all they'd ever really been.

They slept for the rest of that day and all of the night, to Piper's amazement, and awoke to a frost-sparkled morning that had drawn exquisite paisley patterns on the glass in the schoolhouse's few windows.

Sawyer was already up—she could hear him rattling the door of the stove, whistling under his breath.

Smiling, purely happy, she snuggled down in the warmth of the bed, every part of her pulsing with the memory of their lovemaking.

"You'd better get up, Teacher," Sawyer called good-naturedly, from the other room. "School starts in an hour."

Reality jolted through Piper, and she bolted out of bed, immediately beginning to shiver as the cold morning air struck her bare skin. She fumbled for her flannel wrapper and put it on quickly. "An *hour*?"

she called back, padding in to squeeze up close to the stove while Sawyer dumped ground coffee beans into the pot.

It was only then that she noticed he'd removed his sling, though not his bandages, and even as he finished putting the coffee on to brew, he was slowly flexing and unflexing his left elbow.

"What are you *doing?*" Piper demanded, instantly alarmed.

"What I can," Sawyer responded. "I still have a lot of use for this arm, Mrs. McKettrick, and I don't want the muscles to atrophy."

"They *won't,*" she said. "Doc Howard would have warned us, if that were the case. He'd have said—"

"Doc Howard, for all his versatility, is a dentist, not a medical practitioner," Sawyer reminded her, still moving his limb. "We've got a couple of doctors in the McKettrick clan, and any one of them would tell me to start using this arm a little every day."

Piper started to protest, and then stopped herself. Reasoning with a man was one thing, and nagging him was another. Besides, she recognized a lost cause when she saw one.

"These McKettricks seem to be an opinionated bunch," she observed, ladling hot water from a kettle on the stove into a basin so she could wash up before she put on her clothes.

Sawyer's grin flashed. "You'll fit right in," he said.

CHAPTER 10

Afternoon, Christmas Eve

There were so many people in the Blue River schoolhouse, Piper thought happily, that even one more wouldn't fit.

And yet, somehow, there was a place for all the latecomers, with their smiles and words of greeting, their homemade fruit-cakes and fruit pies.

The evening before, Clay had brought a fresh Christmas tree in from the ranch, deeming the first one a pitiful sight, past its prime, and Piper and Sawyer had spent a festive hour transferring the ornaments from the old to the new.

Now, Ginny-Sue's eyes widened as Clay lifted her up to touch the feathered wings of the angel that had magically appeared on top of the tree sometime during the night. "Where did she come from?" the child wondered, in an awed whisper. "She wasn't on the *other* tree."

"I guess it's a miracle," Clay told the child, his gaze on Dara Rose, who stood nearby, glowing as she showed off the new baby to one and all. The special angel was their gift to the children of Blue River. "There are a lot of those going around these days, it seems to me."

Ginny-Sue, still weak but mostly recovered, had returned to school only the day before, a little subdued but eager to be a part of things. Once Clay set her on her feet, she hurried off with Edrina, Harriet and Madeline to get ready for the program, and Piper, standing next to Dara Rose, smiled and offered a quick, silent prayer of gratitude.

There was so very much to be thankful for.

Indeed, this *was* a season of miracles, just as Clay had said.

Sawyer, neatly dressed in garments from his travel trunk and temporarily without his sling, caught Piper's eye and winked.

She drew a deep breath and went up to the place where her desk normally stood—it had been pushed back against the wall so the raised floor could be used as a sort of stage—clapping her hands smartly to get everyone's attention.

The cheerful talk ceased, but in a scattered, here-and-there way, and every upturned face was friendly—except, of course, for Eloise Howard's.

Piper gave the other woman a warm smile, secretly feeling sorry for her, and addressed the group in general. "The children have worked very hard to prepare for today's program," she said, in a voice trained to carry to every corner of the room without screeching. "We all hope you'll enjoy it."

Bess Turner, standing in a corner with a cluster of her "girls" from the Bitter Gulch Saloon, faded flowers clad in fuss and feathers, beamed with pride as Ginny-Sue took her place and began to recite the second chapter of Luke. Her performance was flawless, delivered in a bell-like voice, and afterward, no one stinted on applause.

Even Eloise clapped, after a fashion, soundlessly touching the gloved fingers of her right hand to the palm of her left, still flushed with the singular pleasure of informing Piper, twenty minutes before, that her teaching services would no longer be required after the school term ended in early June.

Piper hadn't minded, given that she and Sawyer had already made plans to make their home on the Triple M, up in Arizona, starting the journey north as soon as school was out and the new and more permanent town marshal had arrived, but she'd pretended to feel a *little* bit bad, for Eloise's sake. Heaven knew the poor woman was hard up for things to celebrate, which was a sad thing in and of itself, since she had a good husband, a lovely child and a comparatively easy life, far more than many other people could even have hoped for.

Bess Turner, for example, now hugging and congratulating her proud daughter, might have been grateful for the kind of respectability and love Eloise evidently took for granted—as less than her due.

With a sigh, Piper put the whole matter out of her mind. There was no changing other people; one had to accept them as they were and proceed as best one could, making allowances wherever possible.

The boys took the stage next, putting on a little skit of their own composition, in which shepherds and Roman soldiers speculated about the unusually bright star in the sky over Bethlehem. The soldiers had swords fashioned from kindling and the shepherds had staffs and feed-sack headdresses and, though brief, the play met with critical acclaim and much cheering.

Edrina played a lively tune on her ukulele next, with Harriet turning the pages of her sheet music for her, importantly competent throughout.

Recitations followed, mostly poetry, and when the last of those had mercifully ended, all the students assembled to sing "Silent Night," as rehearsed over many, many days. Piper was touched when, one by one, voice by voice, some awkward, some remarkably sweet, the audience joined in.

It was time then for the presents—the owner of the mercantile had, as usual, brought along the promised oranges and peppermint sticks.

The children were delirious with excitement, especially Ginny-Sue, who had confided to Piper earlier, in a brief moment of privacy, that she had a Christmas tree at home, too. There were parcels tucked into the branches, and "the ladies" had lent all sorts of baubles and ribbons and even silk garters for decorations.

Piper had been delighted by the image and kissed Ginny-Sue on top of the head, telling her, "You'll have a happy Christmas for sure."

And Ginny-Sue had nodded vigorously, eyes shining with joy.

Now, with the oranges and peppermint sticks dispersed, the adults chatted and indulged in pie and cake and all manner of country delicacies, each family, even the poorest ones, having contributed something.

Bess made her way to Piper's side and tugged at the sleeve of her new blue dress, a ready-made from the mercantile. She'd splurged on it, now that she wasn't saving her money to go back to Maine, along with small gifts for Sawyer, Dara Rose and Clay, and, of course, the children.

"We'll be going now," Bess said quietly. "I just wanted to say thank you for everything you did, you and your man, and to wish you a happy Christmas."

Piper's eyes burned, and she smiled, her response delayed by a few moments because she was suddenly choked up. "You're welcome," she said, at last. "And a happy Christmas to you, as well."

"It's the best one ever," Bess confirmed, with a fond glance at her daughter.

And then she and her bevy of twittering birds left the schoolhouse, surrounding little Ginny-Sue, in her warm coat, hat, boots and mittens, like a royal guard escorting a princess home to the palace.

Piper watched them go from the front window, knowing she would treasure the recollection forever after, while the party went on behind her. They were a *family*, those fancy women and that sweet child and blustery Cleopatra, as loving and tightly knit as any other. They'd come to the schoolhouse, knowing there would be some who looked askance, resolved to watch Ginny-Sue make her recitation and celebrate with her classmates, and they'd even put up a Christmas tree, festooning the branches with what they had, rather than tinsel and colored glass.

If that wasn't love, what was?

Sawyer stepped up beside her. "What are you thinking right now, Mrs. McKettrick?" he asked quietly.

She loved it when he called her that. "That Christmas comes in many forms," she replied, leaning against him a little, and delighting in the strength of his arm as it encircled her waist. Then she turned her head, looked up into his handsome face. "Do you miss your family? Because it's Christmas, I mean?"

"*You're* my family," he said, smiling into her eyes.

She let her head rest against his shoulder for a long moment. "I love you," she said.

"And I love you," he replied throatily, holding her a little tighter. Then, in a mischievous whisper, he added, "Let's hurry this party along a little. The sooner it's over, the sooner we'll be alone."

Piper smiled. "We're going to the ranch with Dara Rose and Clay and the children, remember? We won't really be alone until after Christmas, when we move into the marshal's house."

Sawyer grinned and gave her a surreptitious pinch on a part of her anatomy he particularly favored. "Clay and Dara Rose have a big house," he reminded her, "and I made sure we got a room well away from everybody else's."

She flushed. "You're a scoundrel," she accused, though she was pleased at the prospect.

"And you wouldn't have me any other way," he answered.

She laughed in agreement.

With that, they rejoined the festivities.

THE RIDE TO the ranch in Clay's largest hay-wagon was long and cold, and Piper, bundled up in quilts and blankets in back, with Dara Rose holding the well-wrapped baby, Edrina and Harriet all sitting with her in a bed of fragrant straw, wouldn't have changed a thing about the experience.

It was already perfect, just as it was.

Clay and Sawyer sat up front, Clay at the reins of a four-horse team, and as they traveled, the stars started popping out in the blue-black sky, to the delighted fascination of the two little girls. Edrina and Harriet's cheeks glowed, and their eyes danced with happiness and anticipation.

The trail was rough and rutted, the wagon jostled along, and Piper was lulled into a brief revelry by the steady clomp-clomp-clomp of the horses' hooves.

Conversation, it seemed, would be too much effort, at least for the women—the men were discussing something, up there in the wagon-box, and Edrina and Harriet chattered like eager little swallows in springtime—but Piper, for her part, was content just to be with them all.

It was later in the evening, long after they'd arrived at the ranch house, to which Dara Rose and Clay were already adding rooms, when the women finally got a chance to talk. They'd had a big supper, a boisterous affair replete with all sorts of food, and Edrina and Harriet had hung their stockings on the living room mantel and gone to bed with no fuss or delay. Dara

Rose had retreated to nurse the baby and tuck him into his cradle near the kitchen table, where they sat, now that she'd returned. Clay liked to build things, when he had the time, and baby Jeb had several cradles, in various parts of the house.

The men had gone to the barn right after supper, and they weren't back yet.

"You seem happy, Piper," Dara Rose ventured gently. She was a pretty woman, with blond hair, like her daughters', and lively eyes, full of joyful intelligence. "Are you? Truly, I mean?"

Piper blushed slightly, and then nodded. "Yes," she said. "I'm *very* happy. I'll miss you, though. When Sawyer and I move to Arizona, I mean."

"We'll write often," Dara Rose promised, reaching out to pat Piper's hand. "And when the baby is older, we'll come for a long visit." The house was warm, being well-insulated, unlike the schoolhouse, with a wood-burning furnace and intermittent electrical services. There were several fireplaces, and the kitchen stove was a magnificent thing, with a hot-water reservoir that could be accessed by a spigot.

"Sawyer says Arizona is a fine place,"

Piper remarked. It had been a while since she'd seen Dara Rose, due to distance and pregnancy, and there was so much to say that it was hard to choose a place to start.

Dara Rose nodded. "Finally," she confirmed, smiling. "Clay says his granddad thinks it would have been better if Arizona remained a territory, says there'd be less interference from the federal government that way."

Piper had heard stories about Angus McKettrick, the head of the family, who had originally hailed from Texas. Sawyer clearly idolized the man, though he'd come right out and said his grandfather was three years older than dirt and deaf as a fencepost, so she shouldn't be alarmed if he shouted at her to "Speak up so I can hear you, little gal!"

"I think I'm a bit intimidated," she confessed. "By the family, I mean. There are so many of them, and they're all strong-minded and utterly fearless, from what Sawyer's told me. Why, his own mother used to be a sharpshooter, traveling with a Wild West show."

Dara Rose laughed. "And Miss Mandy," she said, "is one of the *tamer* ones."

"Good heavens," Piper fretted. She had Annie Oakley for a mother-in-law.

"Don't worry," Dara Rose counseled. "I was only teasing. I've met Clay's folks—they came to visit not too long after we got married, traveled all that way by train—and I was real nervous before then. I took a powerful liking to them both right away, and so did the girls." She paused. "Here's the thing about the McKettricks, Piper. Once you marry into the family, you're one of them, for life. Jeb and Chloe—Clay's mother and father—they don't seem to see Edrina and Harriet as their son's step-children, any more than he does. To them, the girls are as much a part of the clan as anybody born with the name. They're extraordinary people, really."

Growing up, Piper reflected, she and Dara Rose had depended mostly on each other, when it came to family. It would be lovely to be part of a large group of kinfolks.

"I just hope they like me," Piper said.

"Believe me," Dara Rose insisted, just as the men came in from outside, accompanied by Clay's dog, "they will."

"Are the girls asleep?" Clay asked, bending to kiss Dara Rose's cheek after hanging up his hat and coat and kicking off his boots to walk about in his stocking feet.

"They're probably pretending they are," Dara Rose said in reply, and all the love she felt for Clay McKettrick showed in her eyes as she watched him lean over the cradle to make sure the baby was warm enough.

Sawyer, dispensing with his own coat and hat—he'd put his sling back on for the ride out from town—crossed to Piper and kissed her ear, sending a fiery shiver through her.

The four of them sat around the table for a while after that, talking quietly while the fire burned low in the furnace downstairs, along with the one in the cookstove. The single bulb illuminating the kitchen blinked on and off periodically, and they used a kerosene lantern in between.

Eventually, Clay went down to the cellar to stoke up the furnace, and Dara Rose lifted their sleeping baby from his cradle, holding him tenderly, his face in the curve of her neck.

"I'll say good-night," Dara Rose told Piper and Sawyer, Sawyer having risen from his chair and drawn back Piper's so she could stand, "and a happy Christmas to both of you."

Piper stepped forward, kissed her cousin's cheek. "Sleep well," she told Dara Rose.

The spare room—Piper had stayed in it before, of course—was on the far side of the house, spacious and comfortably, if simply, furnished. It had its own wood-burning stove, which already crackled with a welcoming fire, but her favorite part of it was the bathroom. Like the one near Clay and Dara Rose's room, which they shared with the girls, this one was well appointed with a pedestal sink, a toilet, and a long, narrow tub made of gleaming porcelain.

Water flowed from a copper tank set into the wall, heated by the small boiler beneath.

Someone, probably Clay, had made sure the boiler was operating properly, and when Piper put the plug in place and turned the spigots, gloriously hot water soon spilled and splashed into the tub.

By the light of the lantern she and Sawyer had brought from the kitchen—there were no electric bulbs in this part of the house—Piper shed her clothes as quickly as she could and climbed in while the water was still running.

She sighed and closed her eyes. "Bliss," she said.

A chuckle from the doorway made her open her eyes again and turn to see Sawyer standing there, watching her. "I'd have to agree," he said huskily.

She didn't think he was referring to the bath, and his words made her blush slightly.

"Join me?" Piper asked. She'd taken regular baths at the schoolhouse, of course, but that had been an awkward proposition to say the least. This was a *real* bath, with plenty of hot water and scented salts in the bargain.

Sawyer remained where he was, giving his head a slight shake. His gaze caressed her as intimately as a touch of his hand. "I'll take a bath later," he replied. "Right now, I'm content to watch you."

She sighed again, a crooning sound of purest contentment, not just with the bath but with the whole of her life, and leaned against the back of the tub, even though the porcelain was chilly where it touched her bare skin, and allowed herself to sink deeper into the rising water. "Nothing," she said, "could be better than this."

Sawyer stepped into the room then, set the lantern on a shelf, and knelt beside the bathtub. "Is that a fact?" he asked, holding out his right arm to her, as he was in the habit of doing when they undressed, and, without replying to his question, she unfastened his cuff link and rolled his sleeve up past his elbow.

He swirled the water around her lightly, splashed some on her belly and her breasts. She quivered as his fingertips brushed those same places, and others, too.

"*One* thing might be better than a bath," Piper admitted, feeling saucy.

Sawyer traced the circumference of her right nipple, again, with a fingertip.

A tremor went through her, with a promise of sweet tumult to follow. She groaned, already surrendering to his caresses, even as the water rose and rose, so warm and soothing. The very marrow of her bones seemed to melt.

Sawyer chuckled at her response; he loved the sounds Piper made when he pleasured her, and he was very good at that.

The tub was full, and he turned off the spigots, reached for a bar of soap.

And he began to lather Piper, gently but thoroughly, washing every part of her, and she gave herself up to the sultry, luxurious sensations of his touch, and of the things he said to her, quiet and strictly their own, almost a private language.

Presently, he leaned over and caught her mouth with his, kissed her deeply, all the while stroking the place between her legs, which had opened for him readily, like always.

His lovemaking always seemed new, and exquisitely daring. He'd taken her standing up in the schoolhouse one moonless night, and even now the memory aroused her almost as much as what he was doing now. She'd taken him into her greedily, crying out in welcome as he took her.

"There's more," he always said to her, after each ecstatic surprise.

"There's more," he said now, getting to his feet and reaching for one of the towels Dara Rose had so thoughtfully provided, along with the fancy soap and the ample supply of hot water.

Wobbly-kneed, Piper stood, let him wrap her in the towel. Stepped over the side of the tub and onto the rug to stand very close to him.

He led her into the warm bedroom, lit only by the light escaping from the edges of the door in the little stove, dried her off, and settled her sideways on the mattress. Easing her onto her back, he kissed her and caressed her for a long time.

She waited, dazed with comfort and anticipation, because when Sawyer said there was more, there always was.

Always.

When he slipped away from her, she tried to pull him back, already wanting him on top of her, inside her, but he eluded her grasp.

And then he knelt again, and parted her knees.

When he took her into his mouth, the most sensitive, intimate part of her, she had to stifle a ragged shout of delight. It was scandalous—it was—

"*Sawyer,*" she whimpered, tangling her fingers into his hair, holding him close to her, pressed hard against her.

His mouth. Dear heaven, *his mouth.* What magic was this? What wild, sweet magic was he working on her?

Without withdrawing from her, he eased both her legs up, setting her heels against the mattress. Her bent knees widened and still he feasted on her, nibbling and tasting, teasing her with just the tip of his tongue until she begged for completion.

One of his hands found her mouth and covered it gently, and that was a good thing, because when satisfaction finally, *finally* overtook her, she was making a primitive sound, part sob and part growl, that would have carried clear to town, never mind to the rest of the house.

Before rising from his knees, Sawyer kissed the insides of Piper's still trembling thighs. Several small, sharp after-releases followed, each one causing her to moan softly and arch her back, as though to find his mouth again.

He arranged her properly in the bed and covered her up. "If Clay hears you yelling like that," he joked quietly, "he'll think I'm killing you and storm the room with a shotgun."

Piper couldn't speak. She was still trying to find her way back to herself, still lost on the outskirts of heaven.

She slept a sweetly shallow sleep, rising to the surface now and then, like some exotic fish. She heard Sawyer running a bath in the next room and, later, felt his weight on the mattress when he climbed into bed beside her. She stirred as, unbelievably, desire reawakened within her, blossoming like some soft-petaled flower.

"Sawyer," she whispered, reaching for him.

He moved on top of her, and she widened her legs for him.

He took her slowly, so slowly, and so deeply that her body instantly responded, even though she was still half-asleep. She began to buckle beneath him, as the first climax seized her, followed by another and then another. They were soft, these releases, and she soared with them as surely as if she'd had wings.

Finally, Sawyer too reached the pinnacle, and gave himself up to her with a long, low groan that seemed to rise from the depths of his soul.

"GET UP!" a little voice crowed. "Get up, get up, get up!"

Sawyer opened one eye, spotted Harriet standing beside the bed, holding up a stocking—one of Clay's, probably—bulging with loot.

"It's *Christmas!*" Edrina piped up, from the other side of the bed.

Piper, buried deep under the covers, murmured something.

"And St. Nicholas was here!" Harriet cried, waving the stocking. "Get up!"

Sawyer laughed. "I thought you didn't believe in St. Nicholas," he said, stalling for time. He wasn't wearing a stitch, and neither was Piper, which meant, of course, that the getting-up part would have to wait until the girls were out of the room.

"Now we've got proof!" Edrina trilled, exhibiting a burgeoning work sock of her ow

A doll's head poked out of the top, flanked by what looked like a toy horn of some kind, brightly painted and made of tin.

"And there was a *note!*" Harriet added, her eyes huge with excitement. "St. Nicholas left us presents *in the barn,* and that's why you have to *get up,* so we can all go out there together and see!"

Sawyer thought of the two spotted ponies Clay had been hiding in the barn for three days now, and grinned. The night before, he and Clay had set the small, fancy saddles out in plain sight, on a bale of hay, and draped the bridles over them. "Go wake up your folks, then," he said.

Piper's head popped out from under the covers, and she smiled sleepily at the girls, yawned a good-morning.

Sawyer would have given a great deal for another hour alone with her, right there in the guest room bed, but he knew he was out of luck, given the combination of kids and Christmas.

"They're *already* awake!" Edrina informed him. "Hurry *up*—at this rate, it'll be New Year's before we get to see our presents!"

"Out," Sawyer ordered good-naturedly.

"Go on," Piper urged the girls, with a twinkle in her eyes. "We'll be up and around in a few minutes, I promise."

Possibly because she was their teacher, as well as their mother's cousin and closest friend, Edrina and Harriet scampered out, shutting the bedroom door smartly behind them.

"Hurry!" one of them called back, over the sound of rapidly retreating footsteps.

Sawyer sighed, got out of bed, and gathered up his clothes. He went into the bathroom to dress, and when he came out, Piper was fully clad and pinning up her hair in a loose chignon.

He kissed her nape. "That was quick," he said.

"Christmas waits for no one," she replied, turning in his embrace to kiss the cleft in his strong chin. "Let's go see what St. Nicholas has left in the barn."

One year later
Triple M Ranch, Indian Rock, Arizona

THE WHOLE CLAN HAD GATHERED at the main ranch house, where Angus McKettrick officiated, from his wheeled chair, over a busy and memorable Christmas Eve. Even Clay and Dara Rose were there, with the children, having traveled all the way from Texas on the train.

Since all the McKettricks would have separate celebrations for their own families the next day, gifts were exchanged after supper, and even after months spent with these people, Piper was amazed by the rough-and-tumble love they bore each other. They'd taken her into their lives and hearts back in June, when Sawyer had returned, bringing a new wife with him, and she'd fallen in love with them, too.

She and Sawyer had stayed with his mother and father, Kade and Mandy McKettrick, at first, while they were building their own house and barn on a little rise with a spring and a broad view of the ranch. Mandy was still trim and agile, though she'd long-since given up sharpshooting to reign over her children and grandchildren, as well as her adoring husband.

Besides aunts and uncles, there were sisters, too, and brothers, and cousins galore.

Piper was still getting to know them all.

Sawyer's Aunt Katie, Angus and Conception's late-life daughter, a particular favorite of Piper's, was married to a United States senator and divided her time between Arizona and Washington. She was bound and determined to see that women got the vote and constantly pestered her husband and his associates to "catch up with the modern world" and do something about the problem.

On this sacred night, Mandy approached her newest daughter-in-law and gently touched her protruding stomach. Piper and Sawyer's first baby was due soon—she'd been hoping for a Christmas birth—but that didn't seem likely, since there hadn't been so much as a twinge of a contraction so far.

"You mustn't overdo, now," Mandy counseled. "We're a pretty overwhelming bunch, we McKettricks, especially when we're all in the same place."

Piper smiled, caught Sawyer's eye and received his smile like a blessing. He was standing next to Angus's wheeled chair, listening while the older man went on about the unfortunate changes statehood had brought.

None of them, in Angus's view, were good.

Sawyer winked, and Mandy, seeing the exchange, smiled at Piper again. "At least sit down," she said, steering Piper toward one of the few unoccupied chairs.

Chloe, a lovely red-haired woman and a teacher, like Piper, approached them, having taken a large and gaily wrapped package from beneath the towering Christmas tree. Katie and Lydia and Emmeline, the other aunts, found their way over, too, all beaming proudly.

Chloe handed the parcel to Mandy, who gently laid it in Piper's lap.

Dara Rose joined them, too. From her smile, she was in on the surprise.

"What on earth—?" Piper asked, near tears.

"Open it," Mandy urged eagerly.

Carefully, her hands trembling a little, Piper removed the ribbon, draping it over the arm of her chair for safekeeping, and then smoothed back the tissue paper.

Inside was a quilt, as wildly colorful as the northern Arizona landscape surrounding them all, exquisitely pieced.

"We all worked on it," Katie said.

Lydia and Dara Rose took the quilt by its ends and unfurled it, so Piper could get a good look at the design. The Blue River schoolhouse had been faithfully reproduced in fabric and appliquéd to the center of what, to Piper, was a work of art. There were children embroidered here and there, frolicking in the schoolyard, and she saw herself standing in the tiny doorway, with Sawyer beside her.

"Sawyer told us he ruined your trousseau quilts by bleeding on them," one of the women said.

Piper's vision was blurred, but she could still make out the words stitched, sampler style, in a rainbow arched above the schoolhouse.

"Piper and Sawyer McKettrick," the thread-letters read. "Blue River, Texas, 1915."

"It's so lovely," Piper whispered. "Thank you."

Mandy leaned down and placed a kiss on her daughter-in-law's forehead. "No, Piper," she said. "Thank *you*, for saving Sawyer's life and for being precisely who you are." Mandy's gaze took in the entire gathering in one swift sweep before returning to Piper's upturned face. "Welcome to the McKettrick family," she finished.

* * * * *